THE SECRET OF PIRATES' HILL

In a series of hair-raising adventures both on land and undersea the teen-age brother detectives pit their wits against some of the most ruthless criminals they have ever encountered.

It all starts when Frank and Joe are skin diving just for fun and the thrill of exploring the undersea world. Suddenly, deep in the waters that flow near the foot of Pirates' Hill, a mysterious skin diver fires a spear through Frank's air hose.

From this moment on, danger is never far away. The very lives of the boys are at stake as they, with the help of their pals Chet Morton and Tony Prito, uncover a mystery involving an old Spanish cannon and a fabulous sunken treasure. Again, Franklin W. Dixon has woven a suspense-filled story that will thrill his many fans.

A rocket was streaking directly toward them!

The Hardy Boys Mystery Stories®

THE SECRET OF PIRATES' HILL

BY

FRANKLIN W. DIXON

GROSSET & DUNLAP
Publishers • New York
A member of The Putnam & Grosset Group

CONTENTS

THE SECRET OF
PIRATES' HILL

CHAPTER I

Underwater Danger

"Don't forget, Frank, any treasure we find will be divided fifty-fifty!" Blond, seventeen-year-old Joe Hardy grinned. He checked his skin-diving gear and slid, flippers first, over the gunwale of their motorboat.

"I'll settle for a pot of gold," retorted Frank. He was similarly attired in trunks, air tank, and face mask, and carried a shark knife. The boys had anchored their boat, the *Sleuth*, off a secluded area of dunes, which ran beneath a low, rocky promontory called Pirates' Hill.

"Here goes!" said Frank as he plunged into the cool waters of the Atlantic. Together, the Hardys swam toward the bottom.

Suddenly Joe clutched his brother's arm and pointed. Twenty feet in front of them and only a short distance from the surface was another skin diver in a black rubber suit. The barbed shaft of a spear gun he held was aimed in their direction!

As the man pulled the trigger, Joe gave Frank a hard shove, separating the boys. The arrow flashed between them and drifted away.

"Wow! What's that guy trying to do?" Frank thought as the diver moved off. "He couldn't possibly have mistaken us for fish!"

Motioning for his brother to follow, he swam toward the diver. But the spearman, with powerful strokes, shot to the surface. Apparently he did not want to be questioned.

Pointing, Frank indicated to Joe, "Up and after him!"

As they popped above the waves, they looked about. The *Sleuth* lay twenty feet away. But the spearman was nowhere in sight.

Frank and Joe lifted their face masks. "Where did he go?" Frank called out.

"Beats me," Joe replied, treading water and gazing in all directions.

Conjecturing that the stranger must have swum slightly beneath the surface and taken off toward shore, the Hardys decided to give up the chase and resume their diving.

"Down we go," Joe said as he readjusted the straps that held the air tank on his back. "But keep your eyes open for that spearman."

"Right."

Again the boys submerged. There was no sign

of the other diver. "He sure got away from here fast," Frank thought. "I wonder who he is."

Long, strong strokes with their rubber-finned legs forced the boys downward through seaweed gardens. Small fish swished in and out among the fronds. Seeing no interesting objects to salvage, Frank signaled Joe to head for deeper water. Air bubbles rippled steadily upward.

Moments later Frank felt a sudden jar and his face mask was nearly ripped off. He clawed desperately to put it back in place, but realized that his air hose had been ripped. Frantically he tried to move up, but unconsciousness swept over him.

Joe, who had seen the whole episode, was horror-struck. Another shaft from a spear gun had zipped through the murky deep. From the vast amount of bubbles rising through the water, Joe knew that his brother's life was in danger.

With powerful strokes, he reached Frank's side. Towing the limp form with one hand, Joe headed for the *Sleuth*'s anchor line, dimly visible in the distance. Working his fins as violently as possible, he fought his way toward it for what seemed an eternity.

Finally he reached the rope and pulled himself to the surface. Joe tore off Frank's headgear, holding his face above the waves. Then he pushed him into the boat and scrambled aboard.

Quickly Joe laid his brother in a prone position and applied artificial respiration.

Minutes passed before Frank stirred. Joe continued his treatment until he heard a moan, then a feeble question.

"Where—? What happened?"

"We were shot at again and you were hit," Joe said, helping Frank sit up.

"The same diver?"

"Must have been. Probably he was hiding behind an underwater rock," Joe replied.

"That guy must be crazy!" Frank said, after filling his lungs with deep drafts of air.

"I can't figure him out," Joe mused. "Do you suppose he's looking for sunken treasure and wanted to keep us away?"

"I never heard anybody talk about sunken treasure off Bayport," Frank said.

"No," Joe agreed. "Well, pal, I think you've had enough for one morning. Let's go home."

He pulled up anchor and started the motor. Two miles away on Barmet Bay was the boathouse where the boys kept the *Sleuth*. As they turned toward the bay entrance, Joe grinned ruefully. "I wish we could have kept that spear for a clue," he remarked, "but it passed clean through your air hose and disappeared."

"I did notice one thing when we chased the diver," said Frank. "There was a yellow band around that black swim cap he wore."

Frank realized his air hose had been ripped!

"Pretty slim clue. You feeling okay, Frank?"

Frank said he felt a bit nauseous, but otherwise recovered from the shock. "Hey," he added, "there's someone waiting for us at the dock!"

Drawing closer, they saw a man about thirty-five years old. He was tall, broad-shouldered, and had wiry black hair. He stood motionless, his legs braced apart, looking intently at them.

Joe ran the *Sleuth* into the boathouse and the brothers stepped ashore.

"Good morning," the stranger said as they came outside. "My name's Clyde Bowden. I'm from Tampa, Florida. I assume you're the Hardys?"

"That's right," Frank replied as the trio shook hands. "What can we do for you?"

"A detecting job."

"Let's hear about it," Frank said.

The Hardys, star athletes at Bayport High, were the sons of Fenton Hardy. Formerly a crack detective with the New York City Police Department, Mr. Hardy was now an internationally famous private investigator. Frank and Joe often helped their father on his cases and also had solved many mysteries on their own.

Their first big success was *The Tower Treasure,* and only recently they had had several hair-raising adventures in tracking down *The Clue in the Embers.* Now they were excited about the prospect of tackling a new mystery.

"How did you know where to find us?" Joe asked.

"I just left your home on Elm Street," Bowden replied. "Learned from your mother I might meet you here."

"While we stow our diving gear and get into some clothes, suppose you tell us about your case," said Frank.

The boys put their skin-diving equipment in a locker of the *Sleuth*, then pulled on shirts, dungarees, and sneakers.

They listened intently as Bowden explained that he was searching for an early eighteenth-century cannon known as a Spanish demi-culverin. It was supposed to be in the vicinity of Bayport.

"A Spanish cannon in Bayport?" Joe asked unbelievingly.

"Although I'm not in a position to tell you how I know about the cannon, I'm certain that with your assistance I can locate it," Bowden answered.

As they drove toward the Hardy home, Frank asked the man for the dimensions of the cannon. Bowden described it as being nine feet long and weighing 3,200 pounds. "It fires an eight-pound shot," he added.

"What do you want the old cannon for?" Joe asked.

Bowden smiled. "Believe it or not, I'm helping

to outfit the pirate boats to be used in the famous Gasparilla Exposition in Tampa this year," he replied. "All the details, including the guns, must be authentic."

"That's very interesting," said Frank as they turned a corner toward the town square. "I should think that the type of cannon you're looking for would be found somewhere around the Caribbean rather than this far north. I've read that many Spanish ships were wrecked—"

Frank stopped speaking as a deafening boom suddenly shook the air.

"What was that?" Bowden gasped.

"It came from the square," Frank replied. "Sounds like trouble. Come on!"

Frank drove quickly around another corner and parked the car. They all jumped out.

CHAPTER II

A Suspicious Client

WITH Bowden trailing behind, Frank and Joe sprinted toward a crowd of people milling in the town square. They were gathered around an old Civil War mortar that stood on a pedestal. White smoke drifted from the muzzle.

"Somebody fired the gun!" Joe cried out.

"It must have been an accident," Frank said.

As the boys shouldered their way through the crowd they saw Officers Smuff and Riley of the local police force being besieged with questions from the onlookers.

Before the policemen could reply, a booming voice sounded above the babble and a short, grizzled old man, dressed in a revolutionary Minute Man's costume, complete with tricorn hat and leggings, strode up beside the mortar.

"I can't understand what all this here fussin is about," he said in a booming voice.

He smiled and his weather-beaten face creased into long lines. He told Officer Riley that he was Jim Tilton, a retired artillery sergeant. He had been asked by Police Chief Collig to take charge of the Independence Day cannon salute.

"But this isn't July fourth!" Riley protested. "It's only the first."

The old-timer raised his hands good-naturedly. "I'm mighty sorry I caused so much fuss. After all, I wasn't usin' a ball. I just had some powder an' waddin' in her."

Tilton pulled a letter from his pocket and showed it to the officers. It was from Police Chief Collig and the Fourth-of-July Committee, granting permission for Tilton to test the mortar.

"Well, there was no harm done," Riley said. "Now we know the gun is ready—we and everybody for five miles around!"

Reassured, the crowd dispersed. Sergeant Tilton remained near the mortar, talking with a few men. The Hardys moved closer to get a better look at the old sergeant and the equipment he had been using.

Bowden also edged forward and stared with keen interest at the various markings on the gun. He told the boys that this was a Federal artillery piece.

"It was cast at the same arsenal that turned out the famous Dictator," he said. "That was a thirteen-inch mortar used against Petersburg, Virginia, in the Civil War."

Tilton raised his eyebrows in surprise. "Land sakes," he remarked, "you know a lot! I didn't never suspect anything like that about this ol' hunk o' iron."

As the sergeant began to clean the barrel of the weapon, Bowden turned to Frank and Joe. "My offer to you," he said in a low voice, "is one thousand dollars if you find the Spanish cannon."

The Hardys were amazed. A thousand dollars for an old gun to be used in a pageant!

Sensing their thoughts, Bowden quickly added, "I'm a man of means and can well afford it."

He explained that he had already combed Bayport proper. The boys' responsibility would lie in searching the surrounding areas and nearby towns. Bowden said he was staying at the Garden Gate Motel on the state highway and could be reached there if anything developed.

"We don't charge for our sleuthing," Frank informed the man.

Bowden was astonished. "You've solved all your cases for nothing?"

Joe nodded. "If we should help you," he said, "it will be on that basis."

"Okay. But believe me, I'll make it worth your while somehow!" Then, seeing that Tilton was preparing to leave, Bowden hastily excused himself. "I have a few questions to ask this old codger. See you later."

The Hardys drove to police headquarters to report the underwater attack. They went directly to Chief Collig, a solidly built man in his late forties. He often cooperated with them on their cases, and now listened intently to their latest adventure.

"This is serious," he said. "I'll notify the harbor patrol to be on the lookout for a skin diver wearing a black suit and a black swim cap with a yellow stripe around it."

The boys thanked him and left. As they turned into Elm Street on which they lived, their conversation centered around Bowden.

"It looks as if we're back in business!" Joe remarked. "Let's take on the case."

"I'm a little worried about it," Frank replied. "The whole thing seems a bit phony." He reminded Joe of the many times they had met people who had seemed to be aboveboard, but had turned out to be dishonest.

"It would be fun looking for the cannon," Joe insisted.

"That's true."

At the rambling stone house in which they lived, the boys were greeted by their petite mother and their tall, angular Aunt Gertrude. She was Mr. Hardy's sister, who lived with the family. When she heard about Clyde Bowden's offer, Aunt Gertrude exclaimed:

"A thousand dollars for finding an old piece of junk! There's something underhanded about such a deal. Mark my words!"

Mrs. Hardy's face wore a worried frown. "I wish your father were here instead of in Florida."

"Florida!" Joe exclaimed. "Frank, Dad could check on Bowden's credentials. Let's phone him!"

Mrs. Hardy said the detective could be reached only by mail or telegram at an address in Miami. Frank immediately sent a wire by telephone.

"We may not get an answer for several days," Joe remarked. "I hate to wait. Why can't we make a start on Bowden's case? We can drop it any time we like."

"Okay, but let's not get in too deep until we hear from Dad."

"I'll let Bowden know," said Joe. He dialed the Garden Gate Motel. Bowden was not in, so Joe left a message for him. Then he turned to Frank. "How about advertising in the newspaper for information about the demiculverin?"

"Good idea." By telephone Frank placed an ad in the *Bayport Times*, which had a wide circulation even in the smaller outlying towns.

"I have another thought," Joe said. "Maybe Aunt Gertrude can help us."

"How?"

"As newly elected president of the Bayport Historical Society," Joe said. "she might have some information about ancient cannon in the vicinity."

Their aunt had gone to the kitchen to prepare lunch. Frank and Joe followed and put the question to her. After a moment's thought, Miss Hardy said, "Let me see. I know of one cannon."

"Where is it?" Joe asked eagerly.

"I think it's on the back lawn of a museum in Greenville."

"Do you know what type it is?" Frank asked.

"I believe it may be pre-Civil War," Aunt Gertrude replied. "It might be Spanish. I'm not sure."

"We'll take a look," said Joe.

After lunch the boys set off in their convertible for the Greenville Museum. It was a small building at an intersection of two roads at the edge of town. The main entrance was on one road, with a tall hedge in front of the building. Extensive grounds stretched to the rear on the side road, along which ran a high iron picket fence. Frank parked alongside the hedge, and the young detectives strode through a gate to the spacious lawn at the back.

The cannon, a long-barreled six-pounder, stood in the center of the lawn. Joe dashed across the flagstones leading to it and read the plaque fixed to the piece.

"It's a Spanish gun!"

Frank joined him and read the inscription on the bronze plaque. It stated:

"*Pasavolante*, meaning fast action. Made in Toledo, Spain. Often called *cerbantana*, after Cerberus, the fierce dog of mythology. *Pasavolante* in modern Spanish means peashooter."

"Do you suppose this could be the peashooter that Bowden is searching for and he just got the name wrong?" Joe asked.

Frank looked thoughtful. Then he said, "I doubt it. Bowden seemed sure it was a demiculverin, didn't he?"

Joe nodded. "False clue." He sighed.

As the boys started back across the lawn, they noticed a tall, slender man, with a swarthy complexion, entering from a side gate. He was bareheaded and wore a black leather motorcycle jacket. He looked around as if to make sure that he was not being observed, then moved hurriedly to the gun.

Frank and Joe, casting backward glances, watched him as they continued to the roadway. The man knelt down and read the inscription on the *pasavolante*. Then he rose and walked to the far side of the cannon, scrutinizing it closely.

"Maybe we're not the only ones trying to locate a demiculverin," Joe remarked.

"You're right. Let's go back and question that fellow."

Retracing their steps, they had covered only a few feet when the man suddenly ran for the side gate by which he had entered.

"He must be up to something," Joe said.

The Hardys turned back and hurried to the road. The next moment they heard a motorcycle roar into action.

"I wonder if that's him," Frank said.

Before Joe could comment, the swarthy stranger sped around the corner. Goggles covered his eyes, but his lips seemed to be curled up in a nasty grin. He headed directly toward the boys!

CHAPTER III

A Motorcycle Clue

As the motorcycle roared down on them, Frank and Joe leaped aside and stumbled headlong into the hedge. The driver missed them by inches!

"Sorry," he shouted as he sped off.

The boys picked themselves up. Both were angry.

"I'd like to get my hands on him!" Frank said.

"Did you see his license number?" Joe asked.

"No," Frank answered ruefully. "But the motorcycle looked like a foreign make. I noticed the letter K on the rear fender."

"If we ever run into that fellow again, he'll have a lot of explaining to do," said Joe. "And I'd like to ask him about his interest in the old cannon, too."

"He certainly acted as if he didn't want anyone to know what he was doing," said Frank.

When the boys reached home they hurried into the kitchen. Aunt Gertrude was just removing a batch of cookies from the oven. She glanced over her spectacles and exclaimed, "Frank! You've torn your pants!"

"Had a little accident," he admitted and told her of the motorcyclist.

"I knew it! Hoodlums are after you two again! Well, don't say I didn't warn you." His aunt sighed, then added to herself, "Trouble, trouble everywhere."

"Where else?" Frank asked.

"The Bayport Historical Society," Aunt Gertrude replied. "What would you do with a collection of swords?"

Frank raised his eyebrows. "Swords?"

"Yes, cutlasses. I'd like to keep them."

"Please, Aunty, start from the beginning," Joe begged, "and tell us about it."

Aunt Gertrude explained that the Bayport Historical Society had recently received a gift from the estate of Senator Entwistle. It included some lovely costumes dating from 1812 and a case of cutlasses.

"I argued with our members," Aunt Gertrude went on, "but they insist that we present the cutlasses to the museum at the state capitol."

"Too bad," said Frank, then asked, "Is it your job to have them shipped?"

"Yes. But they are to be moved to the basement temporarily. The museum isn't ready to receive them."

"And you'd like us to help you," Joe said.

"Yes. Tomorrow evening."

"We'll be there," Frank assured her.

The boys went to their room and sat down to discuss the next move in locating the cannon which Bowden wanted.

"We can't do anything today out of town," said Frank, glancing at the radio clock between the boys' beds. "Another hour and it's time for dinner."

"There's something we *can* do," Joe spoke up. "Visit the motorcycle shops in Bayport and find out the name of the foreign make with a K."

"Good idea, Joe. We may even learn the identity of that fellow who nearly ran us down."

The young detectives had better luck than they had anticipated. The first dealer they called on explained that the letter K indicated the motorcycle was a Kesselring, a German make.

"You don't see many of them around," he said. "But they're becoming more popular."

"Do you sell them?" Frank asked.

"No."

"Who does?"

"Nobody in Bayport. And no one in town owns one, either."

"Do you know where the nearest agent is located?" Frank asked.

"Yes," the dealer replied. "In Delmore—155 Main Street. His name is Braun."

"Delmore! That's where the penitentiary is," Joe remarked.

The man nodded. "Braun mostly sells bikes, but he took on the Kesselring motorcycle agency because the machines come from his native country."

The boys thanked the dealer and rode off in their convertible.

"Let's drive over to Delmore in the morning and talk to that agent," Joe suggested.

"Right," Frank agreed. "Incidentally, the main road there is still closed. The detour leads past the Entwistle place where the cutlasses came from."

At home the boys were greeted by the aroma of fried chicken that their mother was preparing.

"You're just in time," she said, smiling.

"Any word from Dad?" Frank asked.

"No," Mrs. Hardy replied. "But we should hear something soon."

Joe questioned Aunt Gertrude about the Entwistle mansion. She said it was supposed to be deserted. "A shame, too, since it's such a beautiful place. One of our Society members hinted that there might be some valuable pieces in the house, so well hidden the executors of the estate didn't find them. He said Mr. Entwistle was a queer old duck. There's even talk that tramps stay there sometimes."

After dinner Frank and Joe decided to ride

out to the Entwistle mansion and look around.

"Maybe we can find out if there's anything to the talk about tramps," said Frank as they drove along the detour road toward the old estate.

"Yes—" Joe began, then broke off as the noisy approach of a motorcycle reached his ears. The next moment he exclaimed, "Hey, Frank! That sounds like the Kesselring!"

His brother listened intently. "You're right. Hope he comes this way."

But the Hardys were disappointed when the sound of the motorcycle grew fainter.

"He must have turned down a side road," Joe said. "Let's try to catch up with him."

Frank was about to agree when both boys saw something that made them gasp.

"That red glow in the sky!" Joe exclaimed. "It's right where the Entwistle mansion is!"

"The place must be on fire!" cried out Frank, stepping harder on the accelerator.

Soon they came within sight of the grounds. On a knoll stood the huge house. One wing was a mass of flames!

"We must get the fire department here before the whole place goes up!" said Frank.

He backed the car around, and in a few minutes the boys reached a farmhouse, where they put in a call to Bayport reporting the fire.

Then they sped back to the scene of the blaze. As they got out of the car, they heard sirens wailing. Minutes later several fire engines screamed to a halt before the burning mansion. Shouts of firemen filled the air while they fought to restrict damage to the wing that was being consumed.

Finally, after a half-hour battle, the flames were quenched and the bulk of the big house stood unscathed. Chief Tally, who had been investigating the charred ruins, returned to his car. A good friend of the Hardys, he greeted the boys with a weary smile. Frank told him they had heard that articles of value might be hidden in the house.

"Could be," the fire chief said. "We suspect an intruder was ransacking the place and dropped a lighted cigarette."

Joe told him of hearing a motorcyclist racing away from the vicinity of the Entwistle place. "He might be the one who was here," he said.

Chief Tally smiled. "You boys are always on the job but this is the quickest I've ever received a clue."

Frank then told him about the man on the Kesselring motorcycle who had nearly run them down. "The machine we heard tonight had the same kind of roar," he said.

"Thanks for the information." The chief nodded, then turned to speak to two firemen who would remain at the mansion, and the boys drove home.

They slept well that night, but the ringing of the telephone early the next morning awakened them. By the time Frank reached the hallway to answer it, he heard his mother talking on the extension in her bedroom. The door was open and she waved him in.

"Fenton, here's Frank now," she said. "You tell him." She turned to her son, excitement in her eyes. "That man Bowden is a fake!" she announced.

CHAPTER IV

New Tactics

"DAD!" Frank called into the phone. "How are you? . . . That's good. What's this about Bowden?"

"The man isn't known here in Tampa, Frank. And no pirate ship with a demiculverin has been entered in the Gasparilla event."

Frank whistled. "I've been suspicious of Bowden from the start. But you don't think we should stop looking for the cannon, do you?"

"Certainly not. Apparently there's a mystery connected with it that's worth checking into. Furthermore, I'm working on a swindling case that Bowden may be mixed up in. I think he's using an assumed name."

"Shall we notify the police or shadow him ourselves?" Frank asked.

Mr. Hardy's advice was to do neither. Instead,

he suggested that his sons continue to be friendly with Bowden.

"It's the best way to get at the truth," he said. "And let me know if I can be of any more help. I'd like to speak to your mother again."

Frank dashed back to the boys' bedroom and told his brother the news.

Joe hopped out of bed. "Frank, this is going to be fun. We pretend to play along with Bowden, but all the time we're trying to find out what he's up to!"

Frank stared out the window. "I'm wondering which problem we should tackle first—Bowden or the motorcyclist."

"Let's combine the two in one trip. We'll go to the motel first, then on to Delmore."

During breakfast with Mrs. Hardy and Aunt Gertrude, the young detectives told about their plan, and as soon as they finished eating, they started for the door. Aunt Gertrude stopped them and handed Joe a book.

"You might as well employ your time profitably while you're riding along. Joe, read this aloud while Frank drives."

Her nephew glanced at the book. "Why, this is great, Aunt Gertrude! It tells about the various types of old artillery. Where did you find it?"

"In your father's library." She chuckled. "I

thought it might give you a clue to that demi-culverin you're trying to locate."

The boys said good-by to their mother and aunt.

"We'll be home in time to move those cutlasses," Frank promised.

As they drove off, Joe turned to a section on culverins and read aloud:

" 'It derives from the Latin word *colubra* (snake). Culverins were highly esteemed on account of their range and effectiveness of fire. Their thick walls, long bores, and heavy powder charges made them the most deadly of fieldpieces.' "

"And Bowden is telling us he wants to mount a fieldpiece on a pirate ship!" Frank muttered.

Joe shrugged. "That's what he's telling *us*. I wonder what he really wants the cannon for."

Half a mile farther down the highway, Frank pulled up in front of the Garden Gate Motel. The clerk told them Bowden was in Room 15.

"There it is!" Joe said, spotting the number. He knocked on the door. There was no answer.

"Hey, this looks like a note," Frank said, eying a paper pinned below the doorknob.

"Maybe it's for us," Joe suggested.

Frank read the message aloud: " *'Bowden! Clear out before it's too late!'* "

"Wow! Our friend has an enemy!" Joe

remarked. "Do you think this will drive him away?"

Frank shook his head. "I doubt it. He wants that cannon too badly. Well, let's go to Delmore and stop here on our way back."

The detour they had to make took the boys past the farm of their friend Chet Morton. Chet was eighteen, roly-poly, good-natured, and loved to eat. Solving mysteries with the Hardys always gave him the jitters. Despite this, he was a loyal assistant and on more than one occasion had rescued them from dangerous predicaments.

"Let's stop a minute," Joe suggested, seeing Chet's sister Iola near the swimming pool.

Frank grinned knowingly. Joe and Iola dated frequently. He pulled into the driveway. The boys got out and walked toward the pretty dark-haired girl.

"Hi!" she said.

"Hello, there," Joe said. "Where's Chet?"

Iola pointed to the pool. Their stout friend was underwater, wearing flippers and a snorkel. He traveled slowly, the snorkel moving like the periscope of a miniature submarine.

"Ahoy!" Joe yelled as they ran to the water's edge.

Chet continued moving about like a walrus. But finally he emerged and removed the face mask and flippers.

"Hi, fellows!" he called. "I'm having a hard time learning this. Can't get down deep enough."

"What's the trouble?" Joe asked. "That extra fat you carry around make you too buoyant?"

"Now, listen here," said Chet, "just because I know good food when I see it—"

Then he changed the subject, telling them he was going to take lessons in skin diving from the same man who had taught the Hardys.

"Swell," said Joe.

"I can't start, though, until I earn enough money to buy all the gear."

"Don't let that worry you," Frank spoke up. "I'll lend you my outfit."

"Thanks. And now bring me up to date on everything that's happened lately."

The Hardys had just finished telling Chet and Iola about Bowden, the mysterious cyclist, and the skin-diving attack, when they saw a car driving in. At the wheel sat Callie Shaw, an attractive girl with blond hair and sparkling brown eyes. She was Iola's friend and Frank's regular date.

Callie alighted, and after greeting everyone, said, "I'm glad you're all here. I wanted to talk over plans for our Fourth-of-July beach party. Tony Prito is coming with us too."

Tony, a schoolmate and fellow athlete at Bayport High, had been through many adventures with the Hardys.

"Let's have a clambake like last year," Chet suggested.

Suddenly Frank grabbed Joe's arm. "Look over there! A man's spying on us!"

He had seen someone peering from behind a tree near the road. The quick glimpse of a black jacket led Frank to believe that the man might be the wanted motorcyclist!

"Come on, Joe!" he whispered, starting to run.

Instantly the man raced off. Having the advantage of a head start, he reached a parked motorcycle, jumped on, and sped off.

From the silhouette of the rider and the sound of the motor, there was no doubt in the Hardys' minds as to the spy's identity.

"It's the guy we're looking for!" Joe exclaimed.

Together, the Hardys ran back to their car and hurried after the suspect. They had covered nearly two miles before they caught sight of him. Reaching the crest of the next slope, he looked back. Seeing that his pursuers were getting closer, he revved his machine and shot into the curving downgrade.

"Faster!" Joe urged. "He's getting away from us!"

Their car whined around the curve in hot pursuit of the Kesselring. Once again they came to a straight stretch of road, but there was no sign of the motorcyclist.

"He turned off!" Joe said in disappointment.

"He must have swung into that dirt road we just passed. Let's go back!" Frank exclaimed.

Screeching to a stop, he made a U-turn and sped to the side road. They plunged onto the rough, narrow, dirt lane. Fresh motorcycle marks were clearly evident. Dust filled the air, choking the boys as they sped along.

"Stop!" Joe cried suddenly. "The track ends here!"

Frank parked the car and locked it, then both boys ran back to the point where the tracks turned off into the pine woods.

"He couldn't go very far through here on his motorcycle," Frank said as they pressed on excitedly.

"You're right!" Joe whispered. "Look!"

CHAPTER V

The Stakeout

AHEAD of the Hardys in the deep woods stood a cabin. The Kesselring was parked near the front door.

Quietly the boys moved into a position giving them a better view of the building.

"Shall we go in?" Joe asked in a low voice.

"I'll go," Frank replied. "You cover the rear, okay?"

"Roger."

Frank walked cautiously toward the front door. It was open and the place appeared to be deserted. The young detective strode inside. No one was in sight!

Frank went out and joined Joe. "He gave us the slip!" he said in disgust.

"But not for long. He'll be back for his bike," Joe said. He suggested that they pretend to leave, then double back and stay in hiding until the man returned.

"Suppose he finds out our car is still on the road," Frank said.

"We'll have to take that chance," Joe declared.

The boys walked off in the direction of their convertible, but five hundred feet beyond the cabin they turned and quietly made their way back. Hiding behind clumps of brush, they began their vigil. Fifteen minutes went by. Thirty.

Suddenly the quiet of the morning was broken by the crackling sound of footsteps.

The Hardys tensed. Someone was approaching from behind them. They shifted their position.

"Get ready, Joe," Frank whispered.

The steps grew louder and a tall figure appeared through the brush. The boys pounced on the newcomer and all three fell hard to the ground.

"Bowden!" Joe gasped.

"For heaven's sake, what ails you guys?" the man stormed, picking himself up.

"We thought you were someone else," Joe replied.

"Why are you here?" Frank asked, wondering if Bowden had a rendezvous with the occupant of the cabin.

"I might ask you the same thing," Bowden retorted.

"That's easily answered," Frank said, pointing

The boys pounced on the newcomer

to the motorcycle. "We want to talk to the man who owns it."

"Do you know him?" Joe asked Bowden.

"Never saw the thing before," he answered.

"Now tell us what brings you here," Frank went on.

"A tip about the demiculverin." Bowden glanced about apprehensively. "It may be buried near here."

Both boys surmised this was another phony story. Bowden was carrying no digging tools, nor was he dressed in work clothes.

"Who gave you the tip?" Frank asked.

"I can't tell you that. The information was given to me in confidence."

Frank was tempted to ask Bowden why he wanted a fieldpiece for a ship. But recalling his father's admonition to play along with the suspect, he merely said:

"Sorry we knocked you down, Mr. Bowden. Let us know if you want us to help dig here."

Joe followed Frank's cue to be pleasant. "We went to the motel to see you this morning," he said. "Frank and I thought we'd talk to you a little more about the cannon you want us to find."

Frank broke in. "We saw the warning note on your door." He watched Bowden closely.

"Warning note?" the man repeated, showing real surprise. After Frank explained, Bowden suddenly laughed. "I guess those kids at the motel were pulling a joke on me. They were playing cops-and-robbers when I left." He glanced at his wrist watch. "I must get back."

He strode off in the direction of the road. Joe turned to Frank. "Do you believe that cops-and-robbers story?"

"No. I didn't see any children around that motel. You know, one of us ought to follow Bowden and send the police up here."

"Good idea," Joe said. "You go; I'll stay."

While he concealed himself to stake out the cabin, Frank cautiously tailed the suspect. "I'll bet we interrupted some kind of meeting," he said to himself.

Bowden walked toward a green Pontiac hardtop parked on the road and roared off. Frank followed in the convertible, memorizing the Pontiac's license number. He was disappointed when the man drove directly to his motel, took the note off his door, and went into his cabin. When he had not come out fifteen minutes later, Frank decided to call Chief Collig and drove to a gas station.

The police chief agreed to send two men to the woods and Frank returned to the spot where he had left his brother.

"Anything doing?" he asked when he arrived at Joe's hideout.

Joe shook his head and Frank told him about

Bowden and Chief Collig. Ten minutes later the boys were relieved by two plainclothesmen.

The Hardys hurried through the woods and drove on to Delmore. It was nearly noon when they arrived at the motorcycle shop.

"Good morning," said the short, smiling proprietor, who introduced himself as Mr. Braun.

"We're interested in Kesselrings," Frank replied. "Do you sell them?"

"Yes, I have the agency. But I haven't sold any motorcycles in a long time. One's been standing in my basement for weeks."

Frank and Joe looked at each other. Was their clue going to lead nowhere?

Joe said, "We'd like to see it."

The three descended a flight of wooden stairs. The man walked around a high pile of cartons, then suddenly exclaimed:

"My Kesselring! It's gone! Stolen!"

Mr. Braun excitedly went on to say that he had been away on vacation for two weeks and had just returned. The Kesselring had been there when he left.

"*Ach,* what will I do?" he wailed.

Frank laid a hand on his shoulder.

"You may get it back this very day," he said. He told of finding the motorcycle at the cabin and of the policemen now at the spot waiting to capture the thief. The dealer was overjoyed.

Frank at once telephoned this latest development to Chief Collig, while Mr. Braun thanked the boys repeatedly. Then they said good-by and left. After a quick lunch at a nearby diner they returned to their convertible.

"Joe, I have a hunch," said Frank. "That motorcycle thief might be a recently released inmate of the penitentiary. Mr. Braun's shop here in Delmore would be a likely place for him to rob. Let's call on Warden Duckworth and ask him some questions."

"Good idea."

The warden was an old friend of Mr. Hardy, and the boys had once assisted him in solving a prison break. Reaching the penitentiary, Frank called him from the main gate phone. A guard accompanied them to Warden Duckworth's office, where the official greeted them cordially.

"What brings you way out here from Bayport?"

Frank told him their suspicions and said, "We'd like to find out the names of men released from here within the past two weeks."

Warden Duckworth rose, walked to his filing cabinet, checked the records, and returned with some cards. "We've let six men go," he replied. "Four old-timers and a couple of young fellows."

"The man we suspect is probably in his twenties," Frank said. "Who were the young ones?"

"One is Bob Chidsie, a car thief. The other, Hal Latsky, a safecracker."

"May we see their pictures?" Frank asked.

"Certainly." Duckworth handed over the record cards, to which small photos were attached.

"That looks like the motorcycle thief!" Joe said immediately, pointing to Latsky.

Frank was thoughtful. "Don't forget, Joe, we've never seen this fellow close up without his goggles. Warden, could you tell us something more about him?"

"Yes—" The man studied Latsky's card for a moment. "Besides being a safecracker, he's an explosives expert. Also, he has an unusual hobby— the study of ancient cannon!"

CHAPTER VI

Mysterious Attackers

AT the mention of Latsky's interest in old cannons, Frank cried out, "That convinces me, Warden! Latsky must be the man we're after!"

Once more the Hardys telephoned Chief Collig, who was amazed by the latest development in the boys' sleuthing. "Are you sure you don't want to join the force?" he asked with a chuckle.

Then he gave them a report on the stakeout in the woods. "Braun phoned in the serial number of the stolen Kesselring," he said, "and our men at the cabin made a positive identification. It's Braun's bike all right. The thief hasn't returned yet, but we'll maintain a round-the-clock surveillance for as long as we need it. Braun has agreed to leave the motorcycle there as bait for the thief. He might try to get it back."

Before the Hardys left, Warden Duckworth

handed them pictures of Latsky. "Give these to Chief Collig," he requested.

On the way to Bayport the boys discussed the strange turn of events. Was Latsky trailing the Hardys because they were searching for an old cannon? Did he know Bowden, and had the two planned a meeting in the woods? Or were they enemies, both looking for the old demiculverin?

"I'm going to phone Warden Duckworth and see if he can tell us anything about Bowden," said Frank.

When the boys reached home, Frank immediately made the call. The warden said he had no released prisoner on his list named Bowden, nor had he ever heard Latsky mention anyone by that name.

"I'll ask the guards and prisoners, though," Warden Duckworth promised. An hour later he called back. "If Latsky knows anyone named Bowden, he never mentioned it here."

"Thanks, anyway," said Frank and hung up.

He was disappointed not to have uncovered another clue but turned his attention to Aunt Gertrude, who had just come in the front door. She was waving three letters.

"I picked these up from the box at the newspaper office," she said, handing them over. "You forgot all about your ad. I suppose these are some answers. Well, hurry up and open them. I'm entitled to know what's inside!"

Frank smiled as he tore open the first envelope. Joe came to stand beside him, and read the letter over his brother's shoulder.

The writer proved to be the amusing old artillery sergeant who had set off the mortar in the town square the previous day. Sergeant Tilton said that he lived up the coast near Pirates' Hill. He had once heard there was an old cannon on the hill, but it had been buried by sand in a storm many years ago—long before Tilton's birth.

Both boys agreed that the lead should be investigated.

The second letter was from Mr. Maglan, the retired custodian of the Bayport Historical Society. Frank opened it.

"Wait till you hear this, Aunty." He chuckled.

"Why, what is it?"

"Mr. Maglan says three old cannons have been stored in the cellar of the Historical Society's building for thirty years!"

"What!" exclaimed Miss Hardy. "Cannons in the basement!"

Joe roared with laughter. "Why, Aunt Gertrude, I always thought you knew everything about the Bayport Historical Society building."

The boys' aunt did not laugh. "This is serious. Suppose there is powder in those guns!" she cried out. "Why—"

Frank assured her that thirty-year-old gunpowder would be damp and harmless. Aunt Gertrude merely said "Humph!" and then reminded her nephews tartly about carrying the cutlasses to the basement. "Mr. Lightbody says they're in the way."

"We'll go right after dinner," Joe said. "And we'll investigate those old cannons at the same time."

The third note was of more serious import. Letters of the alphabet had been cut from newspapers and pasted on the paper to form words. The message bore no signature. It read:

LOOK FOR THE CANNON AT YOUR OWN RISK. IF YOU'RE SMART YOU'LL DROP BOWDEN'S CASE.

"Wow! Things are really getting complicated!" Joe exclaimed.

"Yes," Frank agreed. "And the writer must have found out we're the ones who put that ad in the paper."

"I don't like this!" Aunt Gertrude declared. When Mrs. Hardy heard about the threat, she too became alarmed. Both she and Aunt Gertrude appealed to the boys to drop the case, at least until their father returned from Florida.

"We can't stop work now," Frank objected. "Joe and I are just getting some good leads. And anyway—"

The ringing of the telephone interrupted his

protest. As Joe picked up the phone, everyone waited tensely.

"Maybe it's your father," Mrs. Hardy whispered.

Frank noticed Joe's jaws tighten as he listened. It could not be a call from their father.

"Frank," Joe whispered, "come here! It's Bowden. He wants to talk to you, too."

His brother put his ear close to the phone "Hello," he said, "this is Frank."

Bowden's voice sounded scared. "Listen! You've got to help me! I've been threatened!"

"By whom?" Frank asked. "Those kids again?"

"No, no. This is for real!" Bowden's voice was shaky and faint. But suddenly it became strong again. "Fr-ank! Joe!" he cried out.

"Were you threatened by someone named Latsky?" Frank demanded.

There was no answer.

"Mr. Bowden?" Frank said questioningly.

Still there was no response, but suddenly the Hardys heard a thud and the noise of a phone dropping onto a hard surface.

"Hello! Hello!" Frank kept saying.

There was dead silence for another moment. Then a strange voice said ominously into the instrument:

"You Hardy boys! Drop the cannon search at once! This is your last warning!"

The threat ended with a sharp click as the intruder in Bowden's room slammed down the telephone.

Frank whirled to face his brother. "It sounds as if Bowden had been attacked! Probably by the person who just gave us that final warning!"

Joe started for the door. "Let's hurry over to Bowden's motel. We may catch the guy."

Frank thought it best to get help to Bowden immediately. "He may be seriously injured. I'll notify the desk clerk at the Garden Gate."

With frantic haste, Frank dialed the motel office number, but the line was busy.

"Come on!" Joe urged impatiently. "We can get there in a few minutes if we hurry."

The boys ran to the convertible. When they reached the motel, Frank pulled up in front of Room 15. The door stood ajar and they burst inside.

Bowden lay face down on the floor, unconscious. Blood trickled from the back of his head!

As Joe and Frank rushed over to him, the man groaned slightly and moved his arms. Frank turned him over.

"I'll get some water," Joe offered, and hurried to the bathroom for it. He soaked a towel in cold water and pressed it against the man's neck and face. Bowden shook his head dazedly as he regained consciousness, and the boys helped him to his feet.

"How did you—?" he stammered, recognizing them. "Where's—? . . . Oh, my head!"

Frank assisted Bowden to the bed, where Joe applied an antiseptic bandage he had found in the bathroom medicine chest. Then they began to question him. Bowden said he had not seen his attacker.

"I hadn't locked my door," he explained. "Somebody must have sneaked up from behind and hit me!"

"Latsky?" Frank queried, watching Bowden intently.

"Who's he? Never heard of him," the man said.

"Who threatened you?" Joe asked.

"I don't know. An unsigned note had been shoved under my door. It's right—" Bowden looked toward the telephone table. "Why—it's gone! It was right there!"

"Your attacker must have taken it," Joe said. "What happened to the other note that was stuck on your door?"

"I threw it out. Thought the kids around here were playing a joke on me. Now it looks as if I could have been wrong."

Frank telephoned the desk and reported the assault. The clerk said he had not seen anyone suspicious and promised to notify the police at once.

When Bowden's condition improved, the Hardys tried to ferret out more information from their mysterious client. "Where did you say you live in Tampa?" Joe inquired.

"I didn't say. Why do you ask?"

Joe explained that he thought Bowden's family should be notified in case of serious trouble.

"Forget it," Bowden replied with a wave of the hand. "I haven't any family."

The man's reluctance to tell where he lived seemed to confirm Mr. Hardy's suspicion that Bowden might be mixed up with a group of swindlers.

"About the demiculverin," Frank went on. "I read that it's a fieldpiece and not used on ships."

Bowden was startled for a moment but regained his composure by pulling out a cigar. Lighting it, he said, "I admire your thoroughness. But I didn't want the cannon for a ship, only for a pageant—as part of the shore batteries."

"Oh," Frank said nonchalantly, "then the demiculverin isn't too important."

"What?"

"If it's just for a dummy shore battery, you can rig up a wooden one," Frank added.

"But—but, boys!" Bowden's face grew red with excitement. "I must have the old cannon. Everything has to be authentic."

He laid a firm hand on Frank's arm. "You've got to help me! I'll double the reward. How about two thousand dollars?"

"It's not the money, Mr. Bowden," Frank replied. "It's just that—"

"All right, I'll cooperate better,' he said pleadingly.

"For example?"

"I can't reveal all my secrets, but I feel certain the cannon will be found along the shore here."

"We'll do our best," Frank promised.

When the police arrived, the boys told them all they knew about the attack on Bowden but said nothing about the threat to themselves. Then they left.

"What do you make of it?" Joe asked his brother as they drove away from the motel.

"This mystery is getting more complicated by the minute," Frank replied. "Bowden has an enemy all right, and he's lying when he says he doesn't know who he is."

On the way home the boys noticed another convertible following them. In the rear-view mirror Frank saw that the driver was a good-looking young man in his twenties. He was alone.

"Do you think he's trailing us?" Frank asked.

The car had remained fifty feet behind the Hardys' for about half a mile.

"Why don't you find out? Slow down and see if he'll pass," Joe suggested.

Frank did so. The other driver pulled out and zoomed ahead, staring intently at the Hardys as he passed them.

"Did you recognize him, Frank?"

"Never saw him before."

When they arrived home Aunt Gertrude told them that the Historical Society had just decided to hold a special meeting that evening. "You can drive me over, then move the cutlasses to the basement," she said.

After supper Frank and Joe accompanied Miss Hardy to the Historical Society building. When they pulled into the parking lot in the rear of the old stone building, several members were going in the front entrance.

As Miss Hardy alighted she pointed to a basement window which was open. "Such carelessness!" she sputtered. "I must speak to Mr. Lightbody. Frank—Joe, please close it and lock it when you're down there. Humph! The whole place will be full of stray cats!"

Her nephews grinned as they followed their aunt to the front of the building and went inside.

"The cutlasses are at the rear of that corridor," Aunt Gertrude said, pointing. "Carry them downstairs and don't disturb our meeting!"

Then she walked briskly into the auditorium.

Frank and Joe went down the corridor. At the end of it stood a case with the six cutlasses from the Entwistle estate. Joe lifted out two of the short swords and examined them.

"Boy, the real thing!" he remarked in a low voice. "They're heavy. And look at this edge,

Frank." Taking an old envelope from his pocket he sliced it in half with an effortless motion.

"I'd say these are more dangerous than the cannon," Frank murmured. "Maybe that's why some of the Society members don't want them on exhibit here."

"How about a look at the heavy artillery?" Joe said as the boys replaced the cutlasses in the case.

They looked about for the custodian to show them the basement entrance, but could not locate him.

"I guess we can find our way," Frank said.

He walked over to a door and pulled it gingerly. Instead of leading to the basement, it opened into the auditorium.

Aunt Gertrude was on the dais, gavel in hand. "The meeting will come to order," she said with authority, and the ensuing bang made it plain that she meant every word.

As the members quieted, Frank saw the custodian seated in the front row. He was a small, thin man with gray hair and a wispy mustache. The boys decided not to bother him.

"Let's try this door," Joe said, walking across the corridor. He turned the knob. The door yawned open into pitch blackness.

"This is the basement entrance, all right." He reached inside for the light switch and flicked it on. Nothing happened.

"I guess the bulb's burned out," Joe said.
"I'll get a light from the car, Frank."

He hurried outside and brought back a flashlight which the boys carried with them at all times. As he beamed it down the steps, Frank lifted the case of cutlasses to his shoulders.

"Lead the way, Joe."

Joe went slowly down the cellar steps.

"Careful," he warned. "They're steep."

The next moment he pitched forward. A blow on the side of his head had knocked him unconscious!

"Joe, what happened?" Frank cried as the flashlight flew forward and rolled under a table.

In the feeble glow Frank missed his footing and lost his balance. The case of swords fell from his shoulder and landed with a jangling crash. Frank banged his head on the case and blacked out.

His outcry and the crash of the case threw the Historical Society meeting into an uproar. Mr. Lightbody jumped to his feet.

At the same time Aunt Gertrude pounded her gavel for order. "Keep calm. I'll find out what's wrong downstairs. Come, Mr. Lightbody. Vice-President, please take the chair!"

Miss Hardy charged to the basement door ahead of the custodian and groped her way down the steps. "Frank! Joe!" she called.

She found the flashlight, which was still beaming. Waving it around, she gasped.

Dashing for the open window was a man in a motorcycle jacket, a mask over his face.

In his arms were five cutlasses, which had been hurled from the case. The sixth lay on the floor, next to the motionless Hardys.

Quickly sizing up the situation, Aunt Gertrude reached down for the sword, at the same time crying, "You scoundrel! What have you done to my nephews?"

With a flailing motion, she slapped the man's back with the broad side of the cutlass. He shoved her back.

"Oh, no, you don't!" she cried out.

Thwack! She hit him again. Terrified, the burglar dropped the five cutlasses and leaped to the sill. As he started to crawl through the window, Aunt Gertrude whacked him again!

CHAPTER VII

The Battle of Bayport

THE next moment the intruder was gone. Miss Hardy turned her attention to Frank and Joe.

"Where's the electrical panel, Mr. Lightbody?" she asked.

"Under the stairs." He found it and reported that the basement switch had been pulled, probably by the intruder. The custodian flicked the handle up and the place was flooded with light.

"What happened?" someone called out from the top of the stairs. "Do you need help?"

"Phone the police," said Miss Hardy as she began to chafe her nephews' wrists and the backs of their necks. They soon regained consciousness.

The only injuries the boys had sustained were bruises on their heads. Joe surmised that he had been hit with a blackjack.

After Aunt Gertrude had given a brief description of the assailant, Frank said tersely, "Sounds like Latsky. Let's check for clues to make sure."

As they searched, Mr. Lightbody said the basement windows were always locked. The intruder must have forced one open.

When Chief Collig arrived, Aunt Gertrude told him the story of the attempted theft. "Frank and Joe think it was Latsky," she concluded.

The officer agreed. But a search outside failed to reveal any clues.

The Hardys were still looking in the basement for clues when Chief Collig came downstairs. Suddenly Frank said, "Hey, here's a button from the fellow's jacket!" On the floor near the open window lay a triangular black button imprinted with a motorcycle wheel!

Collig dropped the button into his coat pocket and said, "The motorcycle rider hasn't come back to the cabin yet, but I'm hoping he'll show up soon."

After the chief had left, Joe turned to his aunt. "We haven't thanked you for saving us from further damage."

"Oh, well, somebody had to look after you!" she said, going out the door. "Mr. Lightbody, lock and bar the window. Boys, take those cutlasses. Let's see, where will they be safe? There's a closet upstairs. We'll lock them in there for the time being."

When Mr. Lightbody and the boys climbed upstairs a few minutes later and put away the swords, they found Aunt Gertrude surrounded by members of the Society, praising her for her winning the "Battle of Bayport."

"It was nothing," she insisted. "Now we'll resume the meeting."

All the members followed her into the auditorium except Mr. Lightbody. "I can tell you about a real Battle of Bayport," he said to Frank and Joe.

He explained that in reading pirate lore, he had learned that in 1756 a buccaneer ship had attacked two armed merchantmen off Bayport. One of the trading vessels had been sunk with all the officers and crew lost. The other merchantman had managed to sail away.

"The pirate ship," Mr. Lightbody continued, "had had so much of her sail raked by the cannon of the merchantmen that she was unable to give chase. Instead, for some unknown reason, she sent a landing party ashore. Some time later the party returned aboard and the pirate ship limped off."

"Where did this happen?" Joe asked.

"Off Pirates' Hill," Mr. Lightbody replied. "The hill is really named after that incident."

Frank and Joe eyed each other. Maybe this was the basis for Jim Tilton's account of the cannon buried in the sand!

"That's quite a story," said Frank. "And now

we'd like to see the old cannons in the basement."

Mr. Lightbody led the way down another stairway and unlocked a door to a dusty, vaultlike room. Three old weapons, green with age, were set up in a row on oak mounts.

"All three are British pieces," the custodian said. "They're a *minion,* a *saker,* and a *pedrero.* And they're all made of cast bronze."

"What interesting names!" Joe exclaimed.

"The *saker* was named after the saker hawk, one of the fiercer birds used in falconry. The *pedrero*—you'll notice that it's longer than the others—is relatively lighter because it was used to hurl stone projectiles. The *minion* is the smallest."

"They have beautiful decorations," Frank observed.

The pieces were covered with flower-and-leaf designs. Atop the *saker,* at its balance point, was a handle in the shape of a dolphin.

"This handle," Mr. Lightbody explained, "was used for lashing or lifting the piece. And cannon like these often had colorful nicknames set in raised letters on the barrel."

"This first one is marked *Wasp,*" Joe commented. "The other cannons have no names on them."

The boys studied them for a while, then Mr. Lightbody locked the door and led the way upstairs. Reaching the hall, Frank whispered to

Joe, "That clue to the demiculverin petered out. Let's try Pirates' Hill next."

"Right. We'll go there tomorrow."

Just then Aunt Gertrude, followed by the other Society members, came from the meeting room. The boys' aunt was beaming.

"The Society has just voted to present us Hardys with one of the cutlasses," she told them.

Frank and Joe grinned in delight. "Great!" said Frank, and Joe added, "It'll be a swell souvenir of the Battle of Bayport! Let's take the one you used to scare off the thief!"

He and Mr. Lightbody went to the closet to get it.

The Hardys returned home directly and Joe made a rack for the prized cutlass. Frank hung the weapon on the stairway wall.

"Looks good," Joe remarked. "I think Dad will like it."

As the boys prepared for bed, they speculated about the masked thief's reason for wanting the cutlasses. But they could come to no conclusion and finally they fell asleep.

Next morning after breakfast the boys made plans for their trip to Pirates' Hill.

"Bowden seemed pretty sure the demiculverin's somewhere around there," Frank mused. "Let's try to get a little more information from him before we leave."

He went to the phone and called the Garden Gate Motel.

"Bad news," he said, returning to Joe. "Bowden checked out early this morning!"

Joe stared at his brother. Then he asked, "Florida?"

"He left no forwarding address. Bowden must really be scared of somebody."

Frank and Joe decided to postpone their trip to Pirates' Hill and look for Bowden instead. They would go the rounds of local gas stations, hoping to find that the man had stopped at one and might have mentioned his destination.

They visited one after another without result. As they were about to return home, Joe said:

"Frank, there's a gas station about two miles out of town on Route 7. Maybe Bowden stopped there."

They headed for the place and a few minutes later pulled in. A boy was in attendance.

"Say," Frank said to him, "did a man stop here this morning in a green Pontiac hardtop?"

"Yes," the attendant replied.

"Was he about thirty-five years old, stocky build, and did he have wiry black hair?

"Yes."

Frank said they were trying to find him and wondered where he had gone.

"Said he had a business deal in Taylorville."

Elated, the Hardys grinned broadly and thanked the boy.

"I hope we can make Taylorville before Bowden pulls out of there too," Frank said.

He kept the convertible at a steady pace and they reached Taylorville at twelve o'clock. The town was a fair-sized one, and the streets swarmed with cars and people during the lunch-hour rush.

The boys began a systematic search for Bowden's car, going up one street and down another. After they had exhausted the business area, they started on the residential section.

"I see it!" Frank cried out presently.

Bowden's green hardtop was parked in front of an old-fashioned house which advertised that luncheons and dinners were served there.

"Maybe he's eating," Joe remarked. "Let's park our car around the corner so he won't spot it."

Frank agreed this was a good idea and kept going. He pulled into a secluded, dead-end street and locked the convertible. As they walked back toward the restaurant, Frank suddenly grabbed his brother's arm. "We'd better duck. Here he comes!"

"Where?" Joe asked.

"From that house down the street—the big white one."

They stepped in back of a hedge and watched

the suspect. He went directly toward his car but did not get in. Instead, he turned into the walk which led to the restaurant and disappeared inside.

"What a break!" said Frank. "Joe, you watch the restaurant. I'll go over to that big white house and see if I can find out what Bowden was doing there."

Fortunately the restaurant was almost completely screened from the street by tall trees and shrubbery. There was little chance of Bowden seeing the Hardys.

"You can't just walk into that house and ask about him," Joe said. "Suppose whoever lives there is in league with him?"

"I'll have to do a little acting," Frank agreed. "Pose as a salesman, for instance, and just try to get a conversation going."

"Okay. Now what'll I do if Bowden suddenly comes out?"

"Run for our car and give two blasts on the horn. I'll come over right away so we can follow him."

Frank hurried across the street and rang the bell of the big white house, planning his strategy as he waited.

A thin, white-haired man answered the door. Smiling, Frank inquired if he were Mr. Chestnut. When the man shook his head, Frank asked if he knew where Mr. Chestnut lived.

"Never heard of anybody by that name around here," the elderly man said. He chuckled. "But you came close, son. My name's a tree one, too. It's Ash."

Frank laughed. Then he said, "I'm Frank Harber from the Nationwide Insurance Company. You see, we are introducing a new medical plan and Mr. Chestnut had inquired about it. The girl on our switchboard must have gotten the address wrong. Anyway, since I'm here, would you like to hear some more about it yourself?"

Mr. Ash smiled. "Sorry, but I'm already covered sufficiently. Besides, I just spent all my money. A salesman was here a few minutes ago and sold me some stock."

Frank's heart leaped. He was learning more than he had bargained for!

CHAPTER VIII

Spies

WITHOUT seeming to be too inquisitive, Frank asked Mr. Ash, "Was it oil stock you bought?"

The elderly man shook his head. "It was mining stock. The Copper Slope Mining Company. Ever hear of it?"

Frank said he had and in fact his father owned some.

"I'll bet Dad will be surprised to hear what Bowden is selling," Frank thought, then said aloud, "Where could I find the salesman if I should want to buy some stock?"

Mr. Ash told him the man's name was Bowden and he was staying at the Garden Gate Motel in Bayport. "That's where he told me to phone him if I wanted more."

Frank was so amazed that he almost blurted out the fact that Bowden was no longer at the Garden Gate Motel. He thanked Mr. Ash for his courtesy, then walked quickly down the street. Joining his brother, he told him what he had learned. Joe was equally amazed and puzzled. Though the stock was high grade, Bowden's method of transacting business seemed strange. Both boys surmised that the stock certificate he had given Mr Ash was probably a phony one.

"We'll wait for Bowden and trail him," Frank stated.

It was not long before the suspect came out of the restaurant and got into his car. Frank and Joe dashed around the corner and hopped into their convertible. The trail led toward Bayport, and when they reached the outskirts, Bowden not only turned into the Garden Gate Motel, but went to Room 15, unlocked it, and stepped inside.

"Well, can you beat that!" Joe said.

The boys parked and went into the office to speak to the clerk who had given Frank the information about Bowden's leaving. The man looked surprised.

"I thought you said Mr. Borden on the phone," he explained. "Sorry. Mr. Bowden is still in Room 15."

The boys went to see him and held a casual conversation about Pirates' Hill, saying they were going to start searching that area. Frank asked Bowden if he had any suggestions for them.

"No, I haven't," he replied. "But I'm glad to hear you're going to start work. I don't know how long I can wait around here."

"Are you thinking of leaving soon?" Joe asked casually, hoping for information.

"Oh, not right away," Bowden answered. "But staying here to locate that demiculverin is taking a lot of my valuable time."

"I understand," said Frank. "Well, we'll let you know what we find out."

Since it was too late to search on Pirates' Hill that day, the boys went home. They gathered the various tools which they would use for their digging and put them in the convertible.

"We'll have to take time out from the beach party tomorrow to make a search," said Frank.

Shortly after breakfast the next morning the phone rang. Frank answered the call. It was from Mr. Lightbody. In a highly excited voice the curator cried out:

"The Historical Society building was broken into late last night, and the cutlasses have been stolen!"

"Stolen!" Frank exclaimed. "How did the thief get in? Didn't you secure all the windows?"

"Yes, of course. This time a rear door of the building was forced."

"Joe and I will be right over," said Frank.

The entire family was upset by the news. Aunt Gertrude declared that she was going along.

"I feel a personal responsibility for those cut-lasses," she said.

Miss Hardy and the boys set off at once. By the time they reached the Historical Society building, Chief Collig was there.

"This certainly is unfortunate," he said. "I can't understand how that thief got in here so easily."

"Don't forget, Latsky is a safecracker," Joe reminded the chief.

"Wait a second," Frank said. "Let's not jump to conclusions. We don't know for certain that it was Latsky who broke in here the second time."

Chief Collig agreed with Frank's reasoning. He said he would put extra men on the case and notify the State Police to be on the lookout for Latsky.

"Neither he nor anyone else has shown up at the cabin in the woods," the officer reported. "I believe the fellow knows we're watching the place and won't return."

At that moment there was a loud booming of the old mortar in the town square. Frank and Joe looked at each other and smiled. They had completely forgotten that it was Independence Day! They had planned to watch the parade, then start off for the beach party.

It was eleven o'clock when they reached home. Joe carried the food to the car while Frank consulted a book on tides in the Bayport area. Coming out to Joe, he said:

"I guess we can't take the *Sleuth* after all. The water will be too shallow near Pirates' Hill. It will be low tide in the middle of the day."

"How about asking Tony if we can go in his *Napoli?*" Joe suggested. "It draws much less water than the *Sleuth.*"

"Good idea, Joe. I'll call him." He went to the phone.

"Sure, we can use the *Napoli,*" Tony said. "I'll meet you at the dock."

The Hardys drove off, heading first for the Morton farm. Chet and Iola were waiting for them, with several baskets of food which included lobsters and a sack of clams. Their next stop was at the Shaw house to pick up Callie, then they drove directly to the waterfront.

"Hi!" cried Tony, giving his friends an expansive grin. The *Napoli* was chugging quietly at her berth.

After the food and digging tools had been transferred to the craft and the Hardys had brought their diving gear from the *Sleuth,* everyone stepped aboard and Tony shoved off.

When they reached the end of the bay and turned up the coast, the young people watched for Pirates' Hill. Minutes later they saw it in the distance. The hill was a desolate hump of sand-covered stone jutting into the sea. There was not a house in sight, except one small cottage about half a mile beyond the crown of the hill.

"That must be Sergeant Tilton's place," Frank remarked.

Tony slowed down the *Napoli* some distance off shore and said he was going to test the depth with a pole before going any closer toward land.

"Say, how about my trying out the diving gear now?" Chet asked.

"You can use mine," Frank replied. "I'll help you adjust the equipment."

"I think I'll put my gear on, too, in case Chet runs into trouble," said Joe.

He quickly strapped his air tanks into position and the two boys stepped to the gunwale.

"Hold it!" said Tony. "A guy in a motorboat over there is waving at us frantically. Wonder what's up."

"Who is he?" Frank asked.

"I've never seen the fellow before," Tony replied as the boat hove alongside.

Frank called out to the newcomer, a fisherman about fifty, and asked him what was wrong.

"I'm glad I got to you folks in time," the stranger replied. He spoke excitedly. "I just spotted a giant sting ray near here while I was fishing."

"A sting ray!" Frank echoed in surprise. "Well, thanks for telling us. We'll stay out of the water."

Tony pulled a pole from the bottom of the motorboat and asked Frank to test the depth from the prow of the *Napoli*. Then slowly he steered the boat shoreward.

All this time Joe had been casting his eyes over the large expanse of water. There was no sign of the sting ray. Finally he said aloud:

"Do you suppose that man was trying to scare us away from here?"

"What do you mean?" asked Callie.

"Well, a lot of funny things have been going on lately," said Joe. "It wouldn't surprise me if that fellow had some reason for not wanting us to go into the water."

He found binoculars in a compartment and trained them on the other boat which by now was a good distance away. The craft lacked both a name and Coast Guard identification number.

"That fisherman isn't alone!" Joe exclaimed. "I just saw another man's head pop out from under the tarpaulin!"

"Can you see his face?" Frank asked.

"No. He's getting up now, but his back's turned to us."

"Let's find out who those two men are!" Joe urged.

Tony revved up the motor and the *Napoli*

skimmed across the water. Joe kept the binoculars trained on the mysterious fisherman. Suddenly they seemed to realize that the young people were heading directly toward them. Like a flash the man who had remained hidden before dived under the tarpaulin in the bottom of the boat.

The other man started the engine. Then, in a roar which carried across the waves, the boat raced off.

"Wow!" Chet exclaimed. "Some speedy craft!"

"I'll say it is!" said Frank. "That's no ordinary fishing boat!"

The *Napoli* was fast but not fast enough to overtake the other boat. After a chase of a mile, their quarry was out of sight. Tony turned back to Pirates' Hill.

The boys continued to discuss the men's strange actions until they were almost ashore. Then Chet said, "Let's forget the mystery. If I don't eat pretty soon—"

"We'll take care of that," his sister promised.

Tony anchored the *Napoli* in a scallop-shaped cove, and the young people waded ashore, carrying the baskets of food with them.

"This is an ideal spot for a beach party," Callie said enthusiastically.

She and Iola took charge and gave orders. Frank and Tony were asked to collect driftwood, while Chet and Joe gathered plenty of seaweed. In a few minutes they returned.

"Those stones over there will make a good place for the fire," said Callie.

She had found a natural pit among the rocks. In it the boys piled the driftwood, then lighted it. Soon there was a roaring blaze. Frank heaped more rocks into the fire.

When the stones were red-hot and the flames had died out, they placed a layer of seaweed over them. Then the girls laid the lobsters, clams, and corn on the cob in rows and piled on several more layers of seaweed.

"I can hardly wait," Chet groaned hungrily as he sniffed the tantalizing aroma of the clams.

While the food was steaming, the Hardys brought their friends up to date on Bowden, Latsky, and the search for the demiculverin.

"Later today Joe and I want to climb to the top of Pirates' Hill and look for the cannon," Frank told them.

A few minutes later Iola announced that the food was ready. They gathered around as Joe cleared away the hot seaweed.

"Right this way, folks!" he called out. "First plateful of juicy sizzling hot clams goes to Miss Iola Morton!"

One by one the picknickers came forward and piled their plates. Every clam, lobster, and ear of corn disappeared. Then a huge watermelon was cut into sections and served.

Forty minutes later Chet rolled over on the sand. "I can't move!" he moaned.

"Neither can I!" Joe echoed. "Girls, that was the greatest meal I ever ate!"

There was little conversation during the next hour. Chet was soon snoring and the others stretched out for a rest. But finally they arose and walked toward the water's edge. Chet was the last to join the group.

"How about my doing that skin diving now?" he suggested.

"Okay," said Frank, and helped his chubby friend into the equipment.

"I'll follow you," said Joe, and started putting on his flippers.

Chet lunged forward and stepped into deep water. Almost at once he vanished beneath the surface. Then Joe, too, submerged.

Ten minutes later Chet came up and sloshed to the beach. He removed his face mask and grinned.

"Brought you some souvenirs, girls," he said, and laid a large handful of unusual shells streaked with mother-of-pearl on the sand.

"Oh, they're beautiful!" Callie exclaimed.

Iola clapped Chet on the shoulder. "I'm proud of you, brother. Hope there's a pearl among these."

"How far down did you go?" Tony asked him.

"About twenty feet," Chet stated. "I'll go

deeper next time. And here's something else I found."

From one of his belts he brought out what looked like part of a rusty ice pick.

Tony grinned. "I suppose a whale dropped this. He likes his drinks cold and chips off the icebergs with it."

Chet ignored the gibe. "I'm going to keep it as a souvenir!"

"Joe should have come back by this time," Frank remarked.

Everyone looked toward the water. There was no sign of his brother. Frank became uneasy.

"I'm going to look for Joe," he announced.

Putting on his gear, he hurried into the water and soon was lost to sight. Frank swam up and down the coast off Pirates' Hill but did not see Joe. A sinking feeling came over him. Suppose his brother had been attacked by the ray!

Then a more alarming thought struck Frank. He suddenly recalled the black-garbed skin diver who had speared his air hose earlier that week. Perhaps the man had returned!

Frank struck out faster and peered around anxiously. Suddenly above him he saw a swimmer whose body extended upright. He was clinging to a boat.

"Joe!" he thought, and hurried toward the figure.

His brother was grasping the gunwale of the

Napoli, his face mask removed. Frank surfaced alongside of him and took off his own mask.

"Hey, Joe!" he cried out. "You gave us a scare! Where have you been?"

'Sorry, pal," Joe replied. "I was lying in the bottom of the *Napoli.*"

"Why?" Frank asked in amazement.

"I've been spying on a spy," Joe replied. "Look to the top of Pirates' Hill! See that figure silhouetted up there? He's been watching every move you and the others have been making on the beach!"

"That guy's doing more than watching," said Frank, staring at the lone man on the summit of the hill. "He's digging!"

CHAPTER IX

A Surprising Suspect

FROM where the Hardys were clinging to the *Napoli*, it certainly appeared as if the man were turning up the sand. He held something resembling a blunt shovel in his hands.

"He didn't have that before," Joe stated. "Must have just picked it up."

"Maybe he figured after watching us a while that we weren't about to climb the hill," Frank deduced. "So he feels safe to dig for whatever he's trying to locate."

"He might even be burying something," Joe suggested.

"Well, let's find out what he's up to."

The Hardys donned their masks and swam underwater to shore. Quickly they told their friends about the man on the hill and their desire to see him at close range.

"I suggest that we separate and start looking

for driftwood," Frank said. "Then Joe and I will quietly leave the rest of you and sneak up the hill."

The others agreed, promising not to alert the man by looking up. Joe pointed out a circuitous route to the top which would escape the notice of anyone above.

"You take that way, Frank. I'll wander down the beach and go up from another direction. We'll try a pincer movement on the fellow."

"Okay. I wonder if he's Latsky."

"Maybe he's Bowden."

The picnickers began gathering driftwood, calling out in loud voices which they hoped would carry to the mysterious digger.

Minutes later the Hardys were on their separate ways up the hill. They slipped and slid in the heavy sand. Progress was slow, but finally both reached the crest. Frank and Joe were about three hundred feet apart as they poked their heads above the top and looked around.

The man was nowhere in sight!

Thinking he might be hiding below a hillock of sand, the Hardys walked toward each other, keeping careful watch. They met without seeing the digger.

"Where'd he go?" Joe asked in disgust. "Do you suppose we scared him off?"

"There ought to be footprints."

The boys searched and finally found them.

They were large and far apart, indicating that they had been made by a tall man.

"They go off in the direction of Sergeant Tilton's house," Frank noted. "But the prints can't be his—he isn't that tall."

The marks might belong to Latsky or Bowden, the Hardys decided. Mystified, they followed the prints. Suddenly Joe grabbed Frank's arm.

"If it was Latsky, and if he was the one who stole the cutlasses, maybe he was burying them here until the police alert is over."

The boys turned back and dug as best they could with their hands around the area where the stranger had been standing. But nothing came to light.

"Let's go," Joe suggested. "We're giving that man too much of a head start."

The Hardys hurried along the trail.

Tilton's house, a quaint one-story shingled cottage, stood about three hundred feet away. The hill alternately dipped and rose twice to the high point where the structure was located.

"The footprints lead right to the door!" Frank observed.

Watching to see if anyone might be looking from a window, Frank and Joe walked up and knocked at the door. There was no answer. Frank knocked again. This time someone within stirred. Footsteps sounded and a moment later Sergeant Tilton opened the door.

"Well, this seems to be visitors' day around here!" he said, smiling. "Welcome! Come in!"

"Did you have another caller?" Frank asked, pretending it was just a casual question.

"Yep."

Sergeant Tilton explained that only a short while ago a stranger had stopped at the cottage.

"Where is he now?" Joe asked quickly.

"On his way back to Bayport," Tilton replied. "He was askin' the best way to go."

"Who was he?" Joe prodded.

"Don't rightly know," Tilton answered. "He never said."

"What did he look like?" Frank asked.

"Tall young man. Right nice face. Kind o' greenish eyes an' brown hair. Say, why are you two fellows so interested in this guy?"

The Hardys told Tilton it was because of their advertisement for information about cannon which the sergeant had answered.

"So if any people are going to dig for it on Pirates' Hill," Frank added, "Joe and I want to be the ones."

The man chuckled. "Can't say I blame you."

Frank now told Sergeant Tilton about Mr. Lightbody's account of the Battle of Bayport. "Do you think there could be any connection between that battle and the cannon you think is buried somewhere up here?"

"I sure do," Tilton replied. "There were some crooked dealin's between those old pirates an' certain folks here in those days. I figger mebbe somebody ashore was trying to sell the cannon or trade it fer the buccaneers' loot."

The sergeant suddenly grinned impishly. "I've got a pirate den. D'you want to see it?"

"Pirate den!" Joe exclaimed.

"Yes sirree!" the elderly man replied. "Just follow me."

Though the Hardys felt they should hurry off and try to overtake the young man they wanted to interrogate, they were tempted by Tilton's invitation. A few minutes would not make much difference. Furthermore, they might pick up some valuable information among his treasures.

"All right," said Frank.

Sergeant Tilton led the boys to the kitchen. From an opening in the ceiling hung a rope ladder. The old man grabbed it and thrust his foot into the first rung.

"Up we go!" He laughed. "This is a real genu-wine freebooters' cave I got fer myself up here."

Frank and Joe clambered up after him into the darkness of the room overhead.

"I'll turn on the lantern," Tilton said. "I made this den out of a storage attic. There's no window. But no self-respectin' pirate would want a window in his den, anyway."

He switched on a ship's lantern in a corner of the room. The first thing the boys noted in its dim glow was a pair of cutlasses. For a moment they wondered if the weapons could be part of the stolen collection. But just then Tilton blew a cloud of dust off them, in order to show them to better advantage. They had definitely been in the den a long time!

"Look at those treasure chests!" Joe cried out. "And all those guns!"

The room contained an amazing collection of corsair relics. Coins, rusted implements, old maps, pirate flags and costumes, and faded oil paintings of famous buccaneers decorated the walls and tables. On a rack in one corner hung a variety of old Army uniforms.

"This is great!" said Joe, and Frank added, "I wish we had time to examine each piece. I'd like to come again, Sergeant Tilton."

"You're welcome any time," the man said.

The boys preceded him down the ladder. As they were about to leave, Tilton said, "You know, I plumb forgot to mention something to you. The young fellow that was here a little while ago—he's lookin' for a cannon, too!"

"He is!" Frank exclaimed. "Did he say what kind?"

"An old Spanish demiculverin."

Frank and Joe looked at each other excitedly. They *must* find the stranger!

"Thanks a lot, Sergeant Tilton," Frank said. "You've been a big help."

"Don't mention it. And hurry back fer a real visit."

The Hardys promised and waved good-by. Then, following the large footprints that led away from Tilton's cottage, they hurried on. The tracks led down the side of one hill and up another, but Frank and Joe did not spot their quarry.

At last they reached a point as high as the one on which Tilton's house was situated. Suddenly Joe stopped and gripped Frank's arm. He pointed to a figure in a depression between dunes.

"There he is!"

"Don't let him get out of sight!" Frank urged, running in a westerly direction through the tall grass.

But at that moment the stranger entered the first of a series of deep dips in the sand.

"Oh!" Joe cried out suddenly. His right foot had slid into a hole. As he pitched forward, he felt a searing pain in his leg.

Frank turned and came back. Kneeling beside Joe, he felt the injured ankle joint. "You must have wrenched it. Better not step on your foot. Lean on me."

"Okay," said Joe. He was annoyed at himself. "That ends our little posse."

"Never mind," said Frank. "I'll help you back to the beach and we'll attend to your ankle there."

In their concern over Joe's injury, both boys had stopped looking for the man. Now they peered across the sand hills, but did not spot him.

Moving as fast as Joe's ankle would permit, they neared the picnic spot. A fire was blazing. The Hardys grinned when they saw Chet cooking frankfurters.

"Our friend must have a vacuum for a stomach," Joe remarked.

Frank did not reply. He was gazing intently at a strange young man who was watching Chet and chatting pleasantly with the girls. The fellow, about twenty-eight years old, was very tall, and had a determined, jutting jaw.

"Joe," Frank said excitedly, "unless my eyes deceive me, the man we were chasing has walked right into our camp!"

"One thing is for sure," Joe said. "He's not trying to avoid us now."

"We're not sure he was doing it before," Frank said thoughtfully. "On the other hand, maybe he changed his strategy. He might still want to find out whether we came here to look for a cannon besides having a picnic."

"We'd better be cagey," Joe said.

As the Hardys drew closer, Iola handed the stranger a frankfurter on a roll. A moment later she looked up and saw them.

"Why, Joe, what happened to your foot?" she cried out and ran toward him.

"I twisted it," Joe explained.

"I'm sorry you hurt yourself," Iola went on and added, "We've got company. This is Tim Gorman—Frank and Joe Hardy."

The boys shook hands with Gorman. The same thought went through their minds after they had a close look at him. He was the man who had passed them in a car two days before and had stared so intently at them!

The stranger seemed to sense what they were thinking and mentioned the incident before they had a chance.

"I was looking for someone I know who has the same kind of car as yours," he explained.

Frank and Joe nodded. At the same moment Callie remarked, "Tim Gorman tells us that he has just been to see Mr. Tilton."

"Yes," the visitor said. "I had a very interesting talk with the old sergeant."

"We know," Frank told him. "We were up there too."

"And I just about broke my leg trying to catch up with you on the hill!" Joe declared. "You certainly crossed it in a hurry."

"Really? Why didn't you call?" Gorman replied. "I didn't see you."

The Hardys' suspicious attitude softened considerably. Gorman now offered to work on Joe's ankle. He made an ice pack with a towel and cubes from the picnic basket, and applied it to the swelling. Next, he massaged the joint carefully. In a few minutes Joe said it felt much better.

"Thanks," he said as the man rose.

Frank steered the conversation back to Sergeant Tilton. Gorman talked freely, laughing about the amazing pirate den in the attic and the talkative old man's preposterous stories. But he did not mention the cannon, nor give an inkling of why he had been on Pirates' Hill.

Finally Joe could wait no longer to broach the subject. Bluntly he said, "We understand you're looking for a cannon."

Gorman's face clouded. "I suppose Tilton told you that," he said, his jaw set and his eyes flashing. "That man talks too much. I asked him to keep the information to himself and he told me he would."

"Is it a secret?" Chet asked.

Their visitor looked annoyed, but he regained his composure quickly. "I suppose you might say so," he replied, looking off into space as if trying to decide whether or not to reveal it.

A sudden quiet descended upon the group.

"Joe, what happened to your foot?"
Iola cried out

The Hardys' friends waited for the brothers to carry on the conversation.

Tim Gorman relaxed a little, and said, "I may as well admit that I'm looking for a cannon." He paused. "But I'd rather not say anything more about it."

"As you wish," Frank said politely. "But we might be able to help you. Joe and I have been reading about cannons."

Gorman smiled and said, "I feel it's best that I keep my business to myself. Perhaps later on I could discuss the situation with you."

The pleasant way in which he made the latter statement and the smile which went with it tended to disarm all of the group except Frank and Joe. Though Gorman was friendly, they still felt he was somewhat suspect. Not once had he mentioned a demiculverin, though that was, according to Tilton, what he hoped to find.

"We'll probably see one another," Gorman announced. "I'm staying in Bayport."

Tony Prito asked Gorman if he would like to go back to town with them in the *Napoli*.

"Thanks very much," Gorman answered. "But my car is parked over on the shore road."

He started to say good-by, then suddenly he stopped short and stared at an object in Iola's hand. It was the ice pick Chet had found. She was about to put it in the picnic basket.

Gorman stepped forward. "Where did you get that?" he asked intently.

Chet proudly informed him of his underwater discovery as Iola handed over the pick. The man examined it closely.

"Is it an antique ice pick?" Chet asked him.

Gorman swung about, his face flushed with excitement. "This is not an ice pick. It's a gunner's pick! There *was* a cannon near here!"

CHAPTER X

Fireworks!

TIM Gorman's announcement sent a thrill of excitement through the Hardy boys. There was no question now that a cannon had been on Pirates' Hill. But was it still buried deep under the sand?

Frank was the first to speak. "Have you any idea, Tim, what kind of cannon it might have been?"

"There's absolutely no way of telling," Gorman replied slowly.

Chet had walked up to face their visitor. "How did you know this gadget was really a gunner's pick?" he asked.

"Like Frank and Joe, I've been reading a good deal about artillery," the young man replied. He turned the pick over in his hands and continued, "This is part of a gunner's equipment."

"How was the pick used?" Chet inquired.

Gorman explained that by the eighteenth century, powder bags had come into wide use, replacing the loose powder which had formerly been ladled into the bore of a cannon.

"This made it necessary to prick open the bag inside the cannon so the priming fire from the vent could reach the charge. This tool did the trick."

Gorman smiled. "I'll be glad to give you cannon instruction any time, but I must be off now."

He shook hands with everyone and said goodby. When he was out of sight, Callie said:

"You'd better dig for that cannon pretty soon or Gorman will find it first."

"Let's start right now," Frank urged.

Acting as leader he assigned the others to various spots and for an hour the beach and hillside were beehives of activity. Various small objects were dug up but there was no sign of a cannon.

"I guess we'll have to quit!" Tony called out to Frank. He explained that he had promised to be home for supper by seven and take his parents in the *Napoli* later to see the fireworks.

"We're all going in the *Sleuth*," said Iola. "Sorry you can't join us, Tony."

The tools were collected and carried out to the boat along with the picnic baskets. After everyone was seated, Tony headed back toward town. Frank and Joe sat alone in the prow for a while discussing Gorman. Frank said he was convinced the young man was aboveboard, but Joe was still suspicious.

"He may just be a very smooth operator," Joe remarked. "Why, he might even be in league with Latsky!"

The boys' discussion was interrupted by a call from Callie. "Oh, look, everybody!"

The *Napoli* had turned into the bay and was running close to shore where an area of the water had been roped off for the evening's display of fireworks. A small grandstand had been erected along the bank. In the water two large scows contained the set pieces and the rockets which would be sent skyward during the celebration.

"Looks as if it'll be a good show," Tony remarked.

Chet proposed that they come early in the *Sleuth* and anchor as close as possible to the two barges so they could get an excellent view of the performance.

At eight-thirty Frank and Joe went to their boathouse where Chet and the girls were waiting. Soon the group was aboard the *Sleuth*, heading out to the area where the fireworks were to be displayed. Nearing it, they could hear band music from the grandstand on the shore.

A large crowd was gathered both on the bank and on the water. Small craft filled with onlookers bustled in the harbor, each skipper seeking a good place from which to view the fireworks.

Frank guided the *Sleuth* close to the roped-off area. Floodlights set up on the scows made the scene as bright as day.

As Frank turned off the motor, Joe, seated alongside him, suddenly grabbed his arm.

"What's up?" Frank asked, turning. He noticed a worried look on his brother's face.

"The man who seems to be in charge of the fireworks display is the one who warned us about the sting ray!"

Frank gazed ahead and nodded. "I wonder if the fellow who was hiding in the bottom of his boat is here too."

There was no possible way to find out now. It was two minutes to nine. The man was hastily directing several workers, none of whom was familiar to the boys.

"They're going to start!" Chet called.

A moment later there was a swish and whine as the first rocket was set off. It shot high into the dark sky above the harbor and a fountain of cascading diamonds burst into life. Ohs and ahs echoed from the onlookers.

A second and a third rocket swirled heavenward. Red and blue sparkles gleamed brilliantly after the sharp explosions.

"This is wonderful!" Iola cried out.

"Oh, they're going to set off one of the figures!" Callie said excitedly. "Look, it's a man pedaling a bicycle!"

A twenty-foot figure, sputtering yellow-white smoke, appeared to be cycling across the barge.

"There goes another figure!" Chet cried in delight as a multicolored clown began to dance with slow, jerky motions.

Just then a hissing sound attracted the attention of the Hardys and their friends. The next moment a shriek went up from the girls.

A rocket had been fired horizontally and was streaking directly toward them!

Terrified, everyone in the *Sleuth* sprawled flat, as it skittered over the waves like a guided missile!

Whack! A shudder went through the boat as the rocket glanced off her bow. A thundering blast followed when it exploded ten yards off the starboard side.

Streamers of white light ribboned across the motorboat, but the hot rocket itself sizzled on the surface of the water and then died out in a cloud of acrid smoke.

"That was too close for comfort!" Joe cried out, jumping up.

Frank leaped back to the wheel as Chet, Iola, and Callie sat up and peered over the gunwales toward the barge.

"That was no accident!" Frank stormed. "I'm going after the man who set off the rocket!"

"Pour it on!" Joe shouted.

The motor roared to life and the propeller

kicked up white foam as the *Sleuth* shot ahead and ducked under the rope of the danger zone.

Closing in rapidly on the barge, the Hardys noticed that one of the Bayport Police Department launches was approaching from the opposite side. Its two powerful spotlights were raking the fireworks platform and the officers were shouting that there was to be no more firing.

"Look!" Joe cried. "That guy over there isn't paying any attention!"

A stranger to the Hardys, he grabbed a lighted torch from the hands of the head man and started for one of the rockets.

"He'll blow us all up!" Callie cried in terror.

A second later the young people saw him run from fixture to fixture, touching his torch to the fuses of the entire remaining display.

Frank did not wait. He put the *Sleuth* in reverse, and the motorboat skittered backward.

The next moment the bay shook with the din of the bursting pyrotechnics. Rockets spewed in all directions with thunderous detonations.

The danger of being struck by the flying missiles also drove the police launch back from the barge toward the center of the bay. There were anxious moments as the bombardment continued.

Hot fragments from the bursting rockets sprayed the deck and cockpit of the *Sleuth,* but finally Frank got beyond their range.

The din aboard the barge ended as abruptly as it had begun.

"What a crazy, stupid thing to do!" Joe exclaimed.

"I'd like to punch the guy who set off those rockets," Frank declared.

"You'll have a hard time," Chet said. "All the men on the barges jumped overboard and are swimming to shore."

Frank turned the boat and headed for the beach. The stranger who had caused the uproar was not in sight, but the man who had warned them of the sting ray was still in the water. Frank drew alongside of him and throttled the engine.

"Climb in!" he called.

The man pulled himself aboard. At the same time the police launch picked up several other swimmers. Not one of them was the fellow the Hardys wanted to interrogate. But they began to question their new passenger.

"Who was the guy who started that explosion?" Joe demanded.

"I don't know."

"What do you mean? You were supervising the fireworks, weren't you, Mr.—?"

The man scowled. "The name's Halpen. I was only in charge of the timing," he answered. "The fellows lighted the fuses when I told 'em to. I don't know the name of the guy who disobeyed orders. He just came around before we were ready to start. I suppose somebody hired him. It wasn't any of my business."

Frank was not satisfied with the explanation. He hailed the captain of the police boat and asked if he might speak to the men they had picked up.

"Sure thing, Frank," said the officer.

The captain requested the men to come to the near side of his craft. Frank asked them the name of the worker who had set off the rockets. Each declared he did not know.

Their own passenger grunted. "I guess the guy just butted in for a good time." He eyed the Hardys. "Unless," he went on, "he was an enemy of yours."

"If he was, we didn't know it," Joe retorted quickly. "But he sure is now!"

"I'm getting cold," said Halpen. "Put me ashore, will you?"

"Okay, but first I want to ask you a few questions," Joe spoke up.

"Well, make it snappy!"

"Who was the man hidden under the tarpaulin in your boat this morning!" Joe shot at him.

Halpen's jaw sagged, his composure gone for a moment. Then he said, "You saw him, eh? Well, he was a stranger to me. His boat capsized and I picked him up. He didn't tell me his name."

"But why did he hide under the cover?"

"Afraid of the sun," Halpen answered gruffly. "And he fell asleep."

Frank took up the questioning. "Why did you race off in your speedboat when we tried to overtake you?"

Halpen glared at him. "It was late. My wife was waiting for me. And now, unless you're going ashore, let me get into the police boat so I can go home."

The Hardys were frustrated, but there was nothing they could do. Frank helped the man board the launch, and it took off for Bayport immediately.

Iola grimaced. "I don't believe a word that man said, do you?"

There was a chorus of "No's." Joe said he was going to find out who Halpen was and what he did for a living.

"Probably nothing much," Chet spoke up, opening one of the picnic baskets. "Who wants a sandwich and a soda?"

Everyone did and in a short while all the food was gone. Chet declared that he was still hungry, and upon reaching the Hardys' boathouse, the group set off for a spot frequented by teen-agers.

Immediately the Hardys and their friends went to phone their families that they were all right. Then Joe called the chairman of the fireworks committee, Mr. Atkin. He had just reached home.

"Halpen's harmless but a loafer," Mr. Atkin said in answer to Joe's question. "He manages to get along somehow, doing odd jobs. At one time he worked in a pyrotechnics factory and understands fireworks. He's had the job of setting off the Bayport rockets and set pieces for the last few years. I can't understand what happened tonight."

Joe now inquired how many men had been engaged to work on the fireworks display.

"Let's see," said Mr. Atkin. "Five. Yes, there were five."

"I counted six," Joe stated.

"What?" the man exclaimed. "Then one of them was there without being hired. He probably was the one who caused a near tragedy."

"I'm sure the mysterious Mr. X was the culprit," Joe agreed. Upon returning to the group, he told the others that so far Halpen's story checked. "It's a puzzle, though. I have a hunch he's not to be trusted."

Frank remarked that he was more worried about the mysterious man who aimed the rocket at them.

The thought of their close escape sobered the group. It was not until some of their high school friends stopped at the table and began to joke with them that they shook off the depressed mood, and enjoyed the remainder of the evening.

The next morning, while the boys were dressing, Frank said he thought they should get in touch with Bowden before making a further search. "Since both he and Tim Gorman are looking for the demiculverin, I'd like to know if they're acquainted."

"Let's go!"

"We'll tell him Chet found a gunner's pick along the shore, but we won't mention Pirates' Hill."

"Right."

The man seemed a bit less friendly than usual when they arrived at his motel. Was he suspicious? But when the boys finished telling their story, he smiled. "You're making progress, I can see that. Keep it up. Time is precious."

Bowden had nothing to offer in the way of news. The police, he said, had no clues to the person who had left him the warning note and later attacked him.

Presently Frank asked, "Do you know a man named Tim Gorman?"

Bowden was visibly disturbed by the question. "Gorman!" he exclaimed, his face flushing. "I'll say I know him, but I'm not proud of it."

"What do you mean?" Joe asked.

"He's no good!" Bowden told the boys that Gorman went about posing as a naval man and was wanted by the police for swindling.

"That's hard to believe," Frank said.

Joe, on the other hand, arched his eyebrows and gave his brother a meaningful look as if to say, "I told you so."

Bowden asked them how they happened to know Gorman. Guardedly Frank told of meeting him on the beach. Bowden interrupted the narration several times to inquire about details. There seemed to be something he wanted to know, but was reluctant to ask point-blank.

Finally, unable to suppress his curiosity any longer, he blurted out, "Did Gorman mention the cutlass?"

CHAPTER XI

An Alias

BOWDEN'S unexpected question perplexed the boys for an instant. Then Joe asked, "One of the stolen cutlasses?"

Bowden looked blank. "What stolen cutlasses?"

"You don't seem to read the newspaper," Frank said. "Some swords were stolen from the Bayport Historical Society building the night before last."

Bowden's surprise seemed genuine and the Hardys concluded that he had nothing to do with the theft.

"Well, what cutlass were you talking about?" Joe asked.

"Forget it."

"Look, Mr. Bowden, you can't play hide-and-seek with facts and expect us to do a good sleuthing job for you!"

The man smiled. "No need for you to get hot under the collar. Gorman's hipped on finding a miniature cutlass—says it's a lost heirloom. He puts the question to everyone."

The Hardys thought this was an unlikely story. They left shortly, saying they planned to continue their search for the cannon.

"I wish Dad would come back from Florida," Joe remarked as they rode along. "This case is getting knotty."

"Joe, it had me baffled until just now. But I believe I have the answer," Frank declared.

"What is it?"

"It might sound farfetched," Frank replied, "but the combination of cannons, cutlasses, and the story about the pirates' fight all lead in one direction."

Joe smiled. "You mean hidden treasure?"

"Right. But we'll have to dig up more clues before we can dig up any treasure," Frank said.

Since the boys had to pass near their home to take the road to Pirates' Hill, Frank suggested that they stop and see if there was a letter or phone message from Mr. Hardy.

The telephone was ringing persistently as they entered the house. "Nobody's home," Frank said. "Grab it, Joe."

The boy picked up the instrument in the front hall. "Yes, this is Joe Hardy. . . . Why do you want to see us, Mr. Smedick?" Joe listened for a moment and added, "All right. Frank and I will come immediately."

Joe hung up and turned to his brother. "A guy with a strained voice, named A. B. Smedick, wants to see us at the Bayport Hotel. Room 309. It has something to do with the cannon mystery."

"We'd better watch out. This may be a trap. I suggest we stay in the hall to talk to that fellow," Frank cautioned.

A few minutes later Joe buzzed 309. Presently the door opened. The Hardys gasped. Tim Gorman stood there!

"What's the idea of this?" Joe asked.

"Please step in," Gorman invited. "I'll explain."

"We prefer staying here," Frank said coolly.

Quickly Gorman reached into his coat pocket, extracted a wallet, and took out a paper and a card. He handed them to Frank.

On the card the boys saw the small photograph of the man in a Navy uniform. Joe inspected it closely to see if any touching up had been done.

It was Gorman, all right, beyond any doubt. The paper was a statement of his honorable discharge from the United States Navy two years earlier.

"Please come in," Gorman said, and the Hardys entered the room. Their host locked the door and they all sat down close together.

"I'm using the name of Smedick here for protection against certain people in Bayport who would like to see me harmed," he said in a low voice. Obviously he was afraid that he might be overheard.

Without explaining further, he went on, "I've investigated you boys thoroughly and know you're trustworthy. I'm very eager to have you help me solve a mystery."

"We're pretty busy right now on another case," said Joe, who still felt skeptical about the man.

Gorman looked disappointed. "I'm sorry to hear that. I really need your help."

Frank suggested that Gorman tell them what the mystery was. Perhaps they could work on it along with their other sleuthing.

Gorman pulled a pad and pencil from his pocket and wrote:

MEET ME TOMORROW AT 2 P.M. IN THE BROWN SHACK ON THE DUNE A MILE NORTH OF PIRATES' HILL. I'LL TELL YOU THEN.

The boys read the message. Frank nodded. But Joe, suspicious, said, "Before we go any further, suppose you tell us what you know about cutlasses."

The boy's remark hit Gorman like a bombshell. He sat bolt upright in his chair, and his face flushed. "Please, not now," he said in a strained voice. "Tomorrow. I'll tell you then."

He arose, took a lighter from his pocket, and burned the note. Then he walked to the door, unlocked it, and ushered the boys out.

The Hardys did not speak until they reached their car. Then, as they drove off, Joe burst out, "What do you make of all this?"

Frank said his curiosity was aroused and he would like to go to the shack. "But I'll watch out for any double-crossing."

"Well, we'd better get back to our search for the demiculverin," Joe urged.

"Let's borrow Dad's magnetometer," Frank added. This was an electronic mine detector for locating metals under sand.

They picked up the instrument at their house, then drove to Pirates' Hill.

"Let's do our searching systematically," Frank said. He proposed that they mark off sectors and work along the beach and the dunes, moving slowly up the hill.

They worked steadily until one o'clock. The magnetometer had indicated nothing of importance. The boys sat down to rest and eat the sandwiches they had brought. It was ebb tide and the beach was deserted.

As soon as they had finished, they resumed their work with the magnetometer. Whenever it indicated a metal object under the sand, the boys dug hopefully. As time passed, they discovered a battered watch, a charm bracelet and a cheap ring, along with soda cans and an old, rusty anchor.

"Say, we could open a secondhand store," Joe quipped.

"A junk yard's more like it," Frank said.

By five o'clock they had dug several holes on the beach and part of the hill but had not found any artillery. Unfortunately, the magnetometer short-circuited. It would take some time to repair it, they knew. Weary, they gave up the search.

"At this rate it'll take us all summer to cover Pirates' Hill," Frank remarked, flopping down on the sand.

"Yes, and Bowden's in a hurry," Joe answered with a grin.

They went back to their convertible and started homeward. Soon after dinner the phone rang. It was Chief Collig.

"I have some important news for you," he told Frank, who had answered.

"What's up, Chief?"

"First, I want to tell you that we still have the stakeout posted at the cabin in the woods, but no one has showed up yet."

"Too bad," said Frank.

"Second, the department has been working on the fireworks case. Since you fellows are interested in finding that phony helper I thought you'd like to know we've traced him to a rooming house."

"Where?" Frank asked.

"Right here in Bayport. His name is Guinness. He skipped out just before we got there, but we picked up a clue that may help us locate him. Officer Smuff discovered it in a wastebasket in Guinness's room."

Frank gripped the phone excitedly. "What is it?"

"An address on a scrap of paper," the chief replied. "It reads *A. B. Smedick, B. H.*"

CHAPTER XII

Startling Developments

STUNNED by the information, Frank echoed, "A. B. Smedick, B. H.!"

"Right," said the police chief. "What do you think B. H. stands for?"

"I'm sure that it means Bayport Hotel," Frank replied, "because we talked to a person there by that name."

"What! Well, then, maybe you can tell us where Smedick is now. He checked out."

Frank, amazed to hear this, said he had no idea. "Joe and I are supposed to meet him tomorrow afternoon along the shore. He probably won't show up. But if he does, I'll try to find out if he knows where Guinness is."

"Do that," said Chief Collig and hung up.

As soon as Frank replaced the phone in its cradle, he rushed to tell Joe, his mother, and Aunt Gertrude the news.

"It sounds to me," Aunt Gertrude commented, her jaw set firmly, "as if everybody connected with this Pirates' Hill mystery is a criminal."

"You could be right. At this point I'm beginning to think Joe's suspicions about Gorman might be justified," Frank remarked.

Joe gave a knowing grin. "I thought you'd agree sooner or later."

"Hold on! I didn't say I'm entirely convinced. I'll let you know after we talk to him at that shack tomorrow afternoon."

"If he shows up," Joe added.

Next morning, when the boys awoke, a heavy rain was falling. Jumping out of bed to close the window, Frank remarked, "It doesn't look as if we'll be able to do any searching at Pirates' Hill today."

After breakfast they decided to spend the morning doing some sleuthing on the stolen cutlasses.

"There's a good chance that they may have turned up at some of the antique shops and pawnbrokers by this time," Frank observed.

The boys' first stop was a curio shop near the Bayport railroad station. The visit there was fruitless.

Next the Hardys drove across town to a shabby antique shop, owned and operated by Robert Dumian.

"I had some cutlasses," the dealer replied to

Frank's question. He eyed the boys with curiosity over his bifocal glasses. "It's funny you're wanting them. Yesterday a boy named Gil Fanning—about eighteen years old—brought five cutlasses in here to sell. Told me they were family relics."

"Is he a local boy?" Frank asked, interested at once.

"Yes, he lives in Bayport," Mr. Dumian answered. "On Central Avenue. I paid him twenty dollars apiece—a pretty steep price, but they were the real thing. Five beautiful swords!"

"May we see them?" Frank asked eagerly. The thought that they might be the Entwistle relics caused his heart to beat faster.

"I'm sorry," the dealer replied. "Right after Fanning brought the weapons in, a swarthy-looking fellow in a black motorcycle jacket came into the shop and bought every one! He didn't give me his name."

The Hardys shot chagrined looks at each other. It appeared that Latsky had beat them to the draw! They were dumbfounded by the appearance of Latsky at the shop—assuming that the man in the leather jacket was he. It certainly looked now as if Latsky were not the person who had stolen the cutlasses from the Historical Society's building. Could Gil Fanning have been the thief?

"That's not all," the man continued. "Last

evening, just as I was closing up shop, a stout boy came in here looking for cutlasses. And now you fellows come in asking for the same thing. I am beginning to wonder if there—"

"Did the stout boy give his name?" Joe broke in.

"Yes," Mr. Dumian said, turning to a spindle of notes on his desk. "He wanted me to get in touch with him if any more cutlasses came in. Here it is." He tore a slip of paper off the spindle and handed it to Frank.

The paper bore the name Chet Morton!

"Chet Morton! We know him," Joe burst out. "What would he want with the swords?"

"Search me," said Mr. Dumian.

The boys thanked him and left the shop. They decided to talk to Gil Fanning, then ride out to Chet's house and ask him why he was looking for cutlasses.

"What a muddle!" Frank exclaimed as they went into a drugstore to look up the name Fanning in the Bayport telephone directory. They found one listed at 70 Central Avenue.

Frank and Joe drove there in the downpour and learned that Gil, an orphan, lived with his grandmother. Tearfully the elderly woman said the boy had not been home for a week.

"He's always been hard to manage," she said, "but I knew where he was. This is the first time he's ever stayed away without letting me know where he is."

"Have you notified the police?" Frank asked.

"Oh, no," Mrs. Fanning replied. "Gil phoned he'd be back in a while. Said he had a job and I was not to worry." Suddenly she asked, "But why are you here? Is my boy in some kind of trouble?"

"Not that we know of," Frank answered. "Mrs Fanning, did you give Gil permission to sell any of your heirlooms?"

"Cutlasses," Joe added.

A frightened look came over the woman's face. "You mean swords? We never had any swords. You must be mistaken."

"No doubt." Frank smiled, not wishing to disturb the elderly woman any further. "Well, thank you," he said. "I hope Gil returns soon."

Frank and Joe left, puzzled by the information. After having lunch at a coffee shop, they headed for Chet Morton's.

As they neared the farm, the rain ended. They learned from Iola that Chet had taken his flippers and snorkel, and gone to their swimming pool to practice skin diving.

"Ever since he found that gunner's pick, he's had a great desire to dive for treasure," Iola added, smiling.

Frank and Joe told her about their search at Pirates' Hill the previous day, then went to the pool to talk to Chet about his visit to the antique store.

To their surprise, he was not in sight. At the edge of the pool lay his snorkel and flippers.

The Hardys returned to the farmhouse and told Mrs. Morton and Iola that Chet was not around. Both looked concerned. Mrs. Morton said that he never left without saying where he was going.

"Perhaps he went off with that boy who was here," Iola suggested. She told the Hardys that about half an hour ago a youth about Chet's age had strolled in and asked for him. They had directed him to the pool.

"Who was he?" Frank asked.

"We'd never seen him before," Iola answered. "He said his name was Gil. He didn't give his last name."

Upon hearing this, Frank and Joe told her and Mrs. Morton the whole story of Gil Fanning and the cutlasses.

"If the boys went off together walking, they probably haven't gone far," said Frank. "We'll look for Chet."

The Hardys hurried off. As they rode along, their eyes constantly swept the landscape, hoping to catch sight of their pal. They went for three miles without passing a car or seeing anyone walking along the road. Presently they came to a combination country store and gasoline station.

"I'll go in and phone Mrs. Morton. Maybe he's turned up meanwhile," said Frank, getting out of the car.

Joe followed, hoping that Chet had returned. But when Frank spoke to Mrs. Morton they learned that their pal had not come back and the family had no word from him. Mrs. Morton declared that she was going to call Chief Collig at once.

Leaving the store, Frank turned to Joe. "What do you think we should do? Keep hunting for Chet, or go on to the shack?"

"Let's go on," Joe replied. "The police will do everything possible to find Chet."

As they approached their convertible, Joe gasped and grabbed Frank's arm.

"Oh, no!" he cried out, pointing to the rear tires. Both were flat!

The boys rushed over to the car. Not only were the tires flat, but to their dismay there were huge slashes in them!

"Someone deliberately cut our tires!" Frank exclaimed.

They wondered whether it had been the malicious mischief of some prankster, or whether one of their enemies was pursuing them and had done it to keep them from meeting Gorman.

"We have only one spare," Joe remarked with a groan. "Where can we get a second?"

"Maybe the storekeeper sells tires," suggested Frank, and returned to the shop.

Fortunately the man kept a few recaps in his cellar. Frank found one that fit the car and brought it upstairs. Working together, the Hardys soon replaced the slashed tires.

"It's way after two o'clock," Frank remarked as they went to wash their hands. "I wonder if Gorman will wait."

Joe reminded him that the man might not be at the shack at all. He still mistrusted Gorman and was sure a trap had been laid for them.

"Maybe," said Frank. "Anyway, we'll approach with caution."

Three miles farther on they reached a side road which they figured would take them near the shack. Presently the road ended and Frank braked the convertible to a stop. Ahead was nothing but sand. The boys got out and looked around.

"There's the shack!" Frank pointed to their right as he put the car keys in his pocket.

The ramshackle old building, badly weathered and sagging, stood between two dunes. They trudged toward it through the wet sand, a fine spray from the windswept sea stinging their faces.

"What a dismal place!" Frank exclaimed

Joe nodded. "Perfect spot for a trap. I don't believe Gorman came, Frank."

As they drew closer, they noticed that the front door was wide open. They concluded no one could be inside, for certainly any occupant would have shut the door against the strong winds.

Nevertheless, Frank called out, "Tim! Hey, Tim!"

No answer!

"It's obvious he's not here," said Joe. "And if this is a trap, we're not walking into it. Let's go!"

At that moment the boys heard a muffled cry from inside the shack. Throwing caution aside, they rushed into the building.

The next instant they were seized by two masked men!

CHAPTER XIII

Mixed Identities

AMBUSHED, Frank and Joe fought like wildcats. Their assailants were much heavier in build and held onto the boys with grips of steel. Neither man relaxed his viselike hold for a moment, despite a hard, occasional punch which the Hardys managed to land.

As the boys fought desperately, the face masks slipped off their attackers. The men were strangers to the Hardys.

Joe wrested his right arm free and sent a vicious punch to his adversary's jaw. The man's grip relaxed and he fell back, groggy. This was Joe's chance for escape!

"Here I come, Frank!" he yelled.

But a kick from the other man sent Joe sprawling. In a flash his own antagonist was on top of him. There was little fight left in his assailant

114

but he depended on his great weight to hold the boy down. Joe could hardly breathe.

At this point Frank was giving his opponent a rough time. The man was now gasping for breath. "I'll let him get really winded," Frank thought, wriggling even harder to break loose.

"Hold still or I'll finish you for good!" the man threatened.

"Just try it," Frank grunted defiantly.

He gave another violent twist and almost broke free. But the man retained his powerful hold. An unexpected downward swipe with his stiffened hand caught Frank on the back of the neck and he slumped to the floor.

The man now turned his attention to Joe and helped his accomplice pin him to the floor. They bound and gagged the young detectives, then held a whispered consultation. One of them went into a back room and returned a moment later dragging something in a burlap sack. He slid it into a corner and both men left the shack by the front door.

Frank and Joe heard a muffled groan. *A human being was in the sack!*

The boys concluded it must be Gorman. He, too, had been ambushed! Were the attackers enemies of Gorman working on their own, or were they in league with Bowden? Or perhaps Latsky?

Desperately the Hardys tried to loosen their bonds. Frank found that by wriggling his jaw and rubbing the gag against his shoulder he could loosen it. At once he cried out:

"Gorman!"

As the bundle in the corner moved slightly in reply, they were horrified to see their assailants rush back into the shack. They had heard Frank's outcry. Without a moment's hesitation, they knocked both boys unconscious.

Some time later Joe revived. He was amazed to find that he was outdoors and dusk was coming on. He saw Frank not far away and on the other side of him the captive in the burlap sack.

"We're in a gully," Joe thought as he struggled to rise.

His arms were still tied behind him and the gag was in his mouth. Every part of his body ached. He was lying face up in a puddle of rain water and was soaked.

Frank, still unconscious, was also bound and gagged. His position was precarious; he lay in a deeper part of the ditch with water rushing only inches from his nose and mouth. The stream, swollen by the heavy rain, was tumbling along in torrents.

"Frank will drown!" Joe thought in horror. "I must get him out of here!" He struggled desperately and finally by twisting and turning slipped his gag off. But his bonds held firmly.

"Frank!" he shouted. "Sit up! Sit up! You'll drown!"

At first there was no response, then Frank made a feeble effort to rise. He raised his head a few inches and tried to pull himself up, but he lacked the strength. Exhausted, he slumped back into an even more dangerous position.

"I must rescue him!" Joe said to himself.

He dragged his body through the mud to Frank. Rolling onto his side, he was able to clutch his brother by one leg with his tied hands. Getting a firm hold, he pulled Frank inch by inch from the threatening stream.

It was an agonizing task. The sharp gravel on the edges of the gully scraped Joe's cheeks, but finally he brought Frank to a safe spot. He managed to remove the gag, but the knots on Frank's bonds defied him.

"We'd better give this up," said Joe, "or I may be too late to save Gorman."

"Go ahead," Frank said weakly. His own arms had no feeling in them.

The burlap sack lay only slightly out of water. "Those thugs must have figured on having the three of us drown in the stream. They evidently sent us rolling down the bank, but we didn't go far enough," Joe thought.

Redoubling his efforts, he crawled to the burlap sack and attempted to secure a hold similar to the one on his brother. But the embankment here had a slimy mud surface. With each attempt to haul the sack away from the water, Joe lost ground.

"I'll never get Gorman out this way!" he groaned. "I'll have to get my hands free."

His bonds were as tight as ever. Joe decided to crawl back to Frank and have him work on the knots again. Halfway to his goal, he heard the sound of an approaching car. Apparently there was a road above the gully!

"Help! Help!" Joe cried out.

The car went by and the boy's heart sank. He yelled even louder. To his immense relief, he heard the car slow down. Then it stopped.

A door slammed, and Joe continued his cries for help. Someone came running and leaned over the rim of the gully.

Bowden!

"Joe Hardy!" the man cried out. "What happened to you?"

"Come down here, quick!" Joe yelled, "Untie me! And we must get the others out!"

Bowden, his raincoat flapping in the wind, grabbed the overhanging branch of a nearby tree for support and slid down the embankment.

"There's a penknife in my pocket," Joe told him. "Get it out and cut me loose."

Bowden did so, and together he and Joe freed Frank and assisted him to his feet.

The burlap sack began to move. Bowden

Joe pulled Frank from the threatening stream

jumped back, startled. "For Pete's sake, what's in there?"

"It's—" Joe started to say, when Frank gave him a warning look.

"We don't know," Frank spoke up, "but we figure it's probably a man. Two thugs knocked Joe and me out. They must have put all three of us in the gully."

The boys made their way to the sack. Both were thinking the same thing. What was Bowden's reaction going to be when he and Gorman faced each other?

With the penknife Joe slashed the cords that bound the burlap sack and yanked it open. A cry of astonishment burst from the Hardys. *The prisoner was not Gorman! He was Chet Morton!*

The stout boy, bound and gagged, and wearing only swim trunks, gazed at his rescuers dazedly. It was evident he was weak and in a state of shock.

"Chet!" the Hardys exclaimed, removing his bonds.

As their pal took in great drafts of fresh air, Bowden asked, "Is he a friend of yours?"

"Yes," Joe replied. "We must get him home at once."

"I'll take you there," Bowden offered.

"Thanks. Where are we, anyway?" Frank asked him, slapping and swinging his arms to restore the circulation.

"On the shore road about ten miles from Bay-port. Say, where did you fellows get slugged?"

"Somewhere up on the dunes," Frank replied offhandedly. He felt in his pocket. The car keys were gone!

Bowden preceded the boys up the steep em-bankment. Frank and Joe assisted Chet, who could hardly put one foot in front of the other.

"You'll feel better, pal, as soon as we get you something to eat," Joe told him.

Chet gave a half-smile and nodded. "Awful hungry," he admitted.

Out of earshot of Bowden, Frank whispered to Chet, "We thought you were Gorman."

"Yes," said Joe. "That guy double-crossed us." He looked at Frank. "I guess you're ready to admit now that Gorman is a phony!"

CHAPTER XIV

Chet's Kidnap Story

As the three boys followed Bowden to his car, the man's denunciation of Tim Gorman came back to them. Bowden probably was right, but where did he himself fit into the picture? The Hardys wondered if there were any significance to the fact that he happened to be passing the gully.

"The less we say the better," Frank warned the others.

Reaching the car, Joe got into the front seat, ready to grab the controls should Bowden attempt to turn off the main road and lead them into any more trouble. But the man drove along normally and in silence.

Suddenly Joe cried out, "There's our car parked just ahead!" It had been pulled way over to the side.

Bowden stopped and waited as the Hardys examined the automobile. The keys were in it and nothing had been disturbed. The motor started at once.

"Thanks again, Mr. Bowden," Frank called, as the other boys climbed into the convertible. By this time it was almost dusk. "We'll have to show our appreciation to you by working harder than ever to locate the demiculverin."

Just then they were startled by a sound that resembled a low, muffled groan.

Frank looked around. "What was that?"

"Just the wind in the trees, I guess," Bowden replied as he waved and drove off.

"Well, one thing seems certain," Frank remarked as he pulled out onto the road. "Bowden didn't know anything about the attacks on us."

"On the other hand," said Joe, "those thugs may have been in his employ and he drove out here to see if they had carried out instructions."

"If you're right," said Frank, "he sure got a surprise. And say, what about Gorman? I guess he didn't come to the shack after all."

"But sent those thugs instead," Joe said.

"Listen, you just said it was Bowden."

"Sure I did. I don't know what's going on. I'm completely baffled. And now, Chet, tell us what happened to you."

"Here's the story. It all began when I put an ad in the paper."

"For what?" Joe asked.

"Skin-diving equipment. I wanted to buy some secondhand. Well, this morning a fellow came out to the farm to see me."

"By the name of Gil," Frank said. "Iola told us. What was his last name?"

"I didn't ask him," Chet said. "I was too excited. You see, he told me he represented a man who was willing to sell his equipment cheap."

"What happened then?"

"I was out at our pool when he arrived. His car was parked down the road and he offered to drive me to the man's house to look at the gear. Since he was in a hurry, I hopped in without taking time to change."

"What then?" Frank asked.

Chet related that the boy had stopped the car in a wooded section which he said led to the house. "As soon as I stepped out, a stocky, masked man jumped from behind a tree. In a flash he had me tied up and blindfolded."

"Then what?" Frank asked.

"While I was lying there in the rain, he said, 'What did you do with the cutlass?'"

"'What cutlass?'" I asked. "He kicked me and said, 'You know which cutlass I mean.'"

"I told him that I had been to an antique shop to buy one but had arrived too late. The man didn't have any left. I sure didn't want to tell him about the one you fellows have."

"I'm glad you didn't," said Joe. "Chet, we were at that shop and heard the story. We think the character who bought all the cutlasses was Latsky."

"Wow! That sure complicates things."

"Why did you go to the shop?" Frank asked.

Chet smiled wanly. "I was hoping to get a clue for you on the sword Gorman and Bowden know about."

"Good try," said Joe. "Go on with your story."

Chet scowled angrily at the recollection. "When I wouldn't tell that guy anything, he flew into a rage. I don't know what he hit me with but he sure kayoed me. From that time on I don't remember a thing until you found me in the gully."

Just then the car reached the side road which led to the shack where Frank and Joe had been ambushed. Frank turned into it.

"Hey, where you heading?" Chet asked. "I thought you were going to get me something to eat. I'm weak."

"Ten minutes won't make any difference," Frank replied. "I just had an idea."

"Well, it had better be good," Chet grunted.

Frank said it was possible that the figure in the burlap sack at the shack had not been Chet. Why would his attackers have bothered to take him there and carry him off again?

"The prisoner was probably someone else—

maybe even Gorman," Frank declared, "and he may still be there."

"Listen, fellows," Chet protested. "I don't want to be captured again now!"

"You won't," Frank said. "You'll take the car key and hide in the trunk. Leave the lid open an inch. You can act as lookout and give us the old owl whistle if anyone approaches."

"Okay, that's safe enough."

Frank parked in the same spot as before. The Hardys put flashlights in their pockets and got out. The area ahead was in semidarkness, with the shack standing out like a black block silhouetted against the sky.

Frank and Joe moved cautiously, taking care not to step in the footprints that led away from the shack. Mingled with them were drag marks, no doubt made by the feet of the Hardys as the unconscious boys were removed from the building.

"You take the front, Joe, and I'll go around," Frank suggested.

They separated. Finding no sign of an occupant, they finally beamed their flashlights through the windows. The shack was empty.

In swinging his light back, Joe became aware of something interesting a few feet away. Quickly he summoned his brother and pointed out a depression in the damp sand.

"Someone was lying there," he said, "Face down."

"Well, it wasn't Chet," Frank surmised. "From head to toe the length is a good six feet."

"Look!" Joe exclaimed. "There's an initial here!"

The boys bent over a spot a few inches from the face mark in the sand. Scratched faintly was a letter.

"It looks like a *C*," Joe commented.

"Or perhaps a *G*," Frank said. "It could stand for Gorman."

They assumed that the man, bound and gagged, had made the impression with the tip of his nose. A more careful search of the area revealed footprints and drag marks that indicated he had been taken into the shack, probably in a sack, then later carried off.

The boys trudged back to the shack and again looked at the face impression in the sand. Frank felt it belonged to Gorman.

"I wish there were some way to make sure," Joe said.

"I think there is," Frank replied. "Let's make a mold of this face."

The Hardys often made plaster molds of footprints and shoe prints. They kept the equipment for doing this in their workshop over the garage.

"We'll have to come back early tomorrow,"

Frank said. "In the meantime, we'll protect the impression."

He went into the shack and looked about for something to use as a cover. In one corner was an old box. He carried it outside, and placed it firmly over the sand impression.

"Let's go!" Joe urged.

As they started back toward their car, the stillness was suddenly shattered by the mournful hoot of an owl: Chet's signal that something had gone wrong.

The Hardys broke into a run!

CHAPTER XV

An Impostor

THE hooting was not repeated and the Hardys wondered if Chet were in trouble. They doubled their speed and quickly reached the convertible. No one was in sight.

Joe pulled up the trunk lid. Chet, inside, looked relieved.

"Did you hoot?" Joe asked him.

"I sure did. A couple of guys were here. I heard them coming through the woods, so I gave the signal."

"Where are they now?" Frank demanded.

"Both of them ran back through the woods when they saw you coming."

"Who were they?"

Chet said he did not know. It was too dark to see them well, but neither was the man who had knocked him out. From Chet's description the

Hardys concluded they might have been the men who had attacked them in the shack.

"They didn't use any names," said Chet, "but they talked a lot." He added that upon seeing the car, they had seemed worried, wondering how it got there. "They decided that perhaps the police had brought it there and were using it as a decoy. Just then they saw you coming and beat it."

"It's a good thing they did," said Frank, "or we might have had another battle on our hands."

As the three boys started home, Chet gave a gigantic sneeze. "Those guys'll kill us one way or another," he groaned. "But I'll probably die of pneumonia first."

Joe wrapped a blanket from the rear seat around Chet's shoulders, but the boy continued to sneeze all the way to the farm. By the time they entered the Morton driveway he was having chills.

"Sorry," said Frank. His conscience bothered him that they had not brought their pal home sooner.

"Look!" Joe exclaimed as they pulled up behind a police car. "Chief Collig's here now."

Mrs. Morton and Iola were overjoyed to see that Chet was safe. Chet's mother at once insisted that he take a hot shower and go to bed. She prepared a light supper, topped off with steaming lemonade.

In the meantime, the police chief listened in amazement as Frank and Joe related their experiences.

Chief Collig agreed with the Hardys that the case had assumed serious proportions. "Take it easy, fellows," he advised. "I'll notify the State Police about that shack. I'm sure they'll want to station a man there."

"Joe and I plan to make a plaster cast of the impression we found in the sand," Frank told him. "We thought it might be a good clue."

"I doubt that it will work," said the chief. "But good luck. When are you going to do it?"

"Very early tomorrow morning."

"I'll tell State Police Headquarters."

The chief said he himself would put more men on the case and station a plainclothesman at the Morton farm. As he left the house, Mrs. Morton bustled into the living room to report that Chet had finally stopped sneezing. "He'll be asleep in a few minutes," she said.

Before Frank and Joe left they telephoned their home. Mrs. Hardy answered and was happy to hear that they had suffered no ill effects from their experiences that day.

When they arrived at the house, Aunt Gertrude greeted them with rapid-fire words of advice about staying away from mysterious shacks. "When you've finished supper, go to bed and get a good night's sleep!" she added. "You need it!"

"You're right," said Joe. "Frank and I have a date at six tomorrow morning." He told his mother and aunt what it was.

Mrs. Hardy sighed. "I suppose it won't be dangerous for you to go if a State Police officer is there."

"I'll call you," Aunt Gertrude promised.

The next morning at five-thirty she roused her nephews. "Hurry," she commanded. "Breakfast is ready and cold eggs and toast are no good!"

The boys dressed quickly and went downstairs to find that their mother and aunt had prepared a hearty meal consisting of hot cereal, scrambled eggs, and cocoa.

"The sooner you solve this mystery, the better!" Aunt Gertrude said as the boys ate. "It has me on pins and needles."

"Too bad," said Joe. "But I think we'll be closer to a solution when we make this death mask."

"What on earth are you talking about? I didn't know someone was—"

Frank and Joe laughed and calmed their aunt's fears. Then, becoming serious, Frank said he hoped the person whose face had made the impression in the sand was still alive.

Joe, pushing back his chair, said, "I'll carry the equipment from our lab, Frank, while you get the car out."

Shortly after six o'clock the boys started off, promising to report back home by lunchtime.

"I won't be here," said Aunt Gertrude. "I'm going over to the state museum to a lecture. While there I'll explain about the cutlasses. The trip will take me until ten tonight."

"Happy landing, Aunty!" Joe said with a grin.

It was a pleasant ride in the early-morning fresh air and the sun stood bright over the horizon when they arrived at the dunes. At once they were challenged by a state trooper who stepped from the woods. Frank showed his driver's license and introduced his brother. The man gave his name as Williams.

"Chief Collig said you'd come," he stated. "Go ahead. There's another officer named Winn at the shack."

Lugging the equipment for making the mold, Frank and Joe trekked to the small building and said hello to State Trooper Winn. "Has anyone been here since you came on duty?" Frank asked.

"No. Not a soul."

The box was still in place over the face in the sand. Joe lifted it. The impression was intact.

"Covering that was a good idea," Trooper Winn remarked.

First, Frank used a spray gun and coated the imprint with a quick-hardening fluid. While he was doing this, Joe mixed plaster in a pail. Then he carefully poured it into the sand.

"When that sets, I hope we'll have a replica of the face, clear enough to be recognizable," Frank said.

When the mold was hard, he lifted it from the sand and turned it over. The result was an indistinct blob. Only the chin line was clear.

"Tough luck," the trooper said. "The sand dried out too much during the night."

"Still I'm certain it's Gorman!" Frank said, pointing out the solid, jutting jaw. "He's a prisoner of those hoods!"

Quickly Joe explained the circumstances to the trooper.

"Will you tell all this to Williams?" the officer requested. "He'll send out an alarm over the radio."

"Let's go!" Frank urged.

The Hardys gathered their implements and hurried back to the convertible. Frank told Trooper Williams of their discovery and he notified State Police Headquarters from his car, well hidden in the woods, to start a search for Gorman. When he finished speaking, Williams let Frank use the radio to contact Chief Collig. The officer said he would institute a local search.

"Let's stop at Chet's," Joe proposed as they reached the main road.

"Good idea. I'd like to know how he is. And

he'll want to hear the result of our experiment."

They found Chet in bed. There was no doubt he had a bad cold, but fortunately there was no sign of pneumonia.

The Hardys stayed with him an hour and brought him up to date on their morning's activities.

Chet scratched his head. "Where do you suppose Gorman is?"

Frank shrugged. "A prisoner some place of either Bowden or Latsky. I hope the police find him soon."

Joe, eager to continue their search at Pirates' Hill, rose and said, "Take it easy, Chet. We'll let you know if anything new turns up."

It was noon when Frank and Joe reached home. Mrs. Hardy had a tasty lunch ready. They ate quickly and soon were ready to go out again.

"I'd like to search until it's too dark to dig," said Joe. "Let's take some supper with us."

Frank agreed. They told their mother they would be back around nine and drove to Pirates' Hill.

Working in the damp sand proved to be a hot, arduous task, and before they ate their sandwiches, the boys went swimming. When the sun was about to set, they packed their tools and left.

"Not one clue to that demiculverin," Joe said in disgust.

"But we're not giving up!" Frank declared.

Exactly at nine o'clock the Hardys' car hummed up Elm Street and Frank turned into their driveway. They noticed a dark-blue sedan parked in front of their home.

"A visitor," Joe said. "Wonder who it is."

Pulling up in front of the garage, they got out and went in through the kitchen.

Mrs. Hardy greeted them. "You just missed a friend."

"Who was it?" Frank asked.

"Tony Prito's cousin Ken," Mrs. Hardy replied. "He came for the cutlass, as you requested."

"What!" Frank cried in alarm.

"Tony phoned a little while ago. Said you were at his house and had told them about the sword. Ken would come over and pick it up in a few minutes. So I wrapped it in newspaper and gave it to him. He just drove off in a dark-blue car."

"Mother!" Joe cried out. "That man was an impostor! We weren't there and Tony has no cousin Ken!"

Mrs. Hardy sank into a chair. "Oh, how dreadful!" she wailed.

Frank put an arm around her. "Don't worry. We'll go and find that man!" To Joe he said, "We must get that cutlass back! There might be a clue in it that will tell us what Latsky, Bowden, and Gorman are really searching for."

The boys dashed to their convertible and sped after the thief.

"There he goes!" Joe cried as Frank turned the next corner.

The convertible leaped ahead. Five blocks farther on, the driver of the blue sedan, apparently unaware that he was being followed, stopped for a red light. Frank quickly pulled alongside on his left. The man at the wheel wore a black motorcycle jacket.

"Latsky!" Joe exclaimed.

On the seat alongside the driver Joe saw a narrow, newspaper-wrapped package. The cutlass!

As Joe flung open the door and hopped out, the man turned to look at the boys. His swarthy face twisted into an ugly sneer.

"We've got you, Latsky!" Joe cried, quickly reaching for the door handle.

But the ex-convict was quicker. Gunning his motor, he shot across the street against the red light. Joe was flung to the pavement.

CHAPTER XVI

The Wreck

BRAKES screeched as oncoming cars tried to avoid colliding with Latsky. Joe picked himself up and jumped into the convertible. Frank, gritting his teeth impatiently, waited for the signal to change. When it clicked to green, he took off in hot pursuit of the fleeing sedan.

"I hope Latsky sticks to the main highways," Joe said. "With his head start, we'll have a tough time catching him if he turns into a side street."

Reaching the outskirts of the older section of Bayport, Frank increased his speed. Suddenly, going over a small rise, the boys saw the red glow of rear lights. A car swung to the left into a T-intersection highway that circled wide to the right, by-passing the outlying residential section.

"It's Latsky!" Joe shouted.

At almost the same moment they heard the wailing of a siren close behind them.

"A police car," Joe said. "I guess the officer thinks we're speeding. Slow down, Frank."

The boy eased his foot off the accelerator and the squad car pulled alongside. Chief Collig himself was at the wheel. "Where's the fire, fellows?"

"We're after Latsky," Frank explained, and quickly told of their chase.

"I'll lead the way!" the chief said.

Though the officer drove a special high-powered vehicle, Joe doubted that he could catch the fleeing car. Latsky had too much of a head start. "Frank," he suggested, "how about taking the shortcut past the old Pell farm? Then we'll come back onto the main highway and throw up a roadblock."

"Great! I'll try it."

Frank whirled to the right at the next lane, roared over a narrow macadam road for a mile, and then turned left into another dirt lane. Minutes later he zoomed onto the highway again.

"Here he comes!" Joe cried out as two headlights flashed over a low hill behind them. In the distance the whine of the police siren sounded.

Frank slammed on his brakes and angled the convertible across the road, so that the red lights blinked a warning to stop. Both boys jumped out, concealing themselves behind a tree along the roadside.

"Wow!" Joe whispered. "Latsky and the chief must be doing ninety!"

The next second there was a squeal of rubber on concrete. Latsky had spotted the roadblock and jammed on the brakes.

"He's out of control!" Frank cried.

The oncoming car headed wildly for the tree behind which the Hardys had taken cover. As they ran, the car bounced off the tree and screeched across the road into a field, where it overturned.

Joe and Frank sped toward the wreck, flashlights in hand. While they were still some distance away they saw Latsky, carrying the cutlass, stumble from the car. Dazed for the moment, the man staggered, but quickly regained his equilibrium and dashed off into the darkness of a woods.

At that moment Chief Collig roared up and stopped. Seeing the flashlights, he got out and hurried across the field. The Hardys were trying to pick up Latsky's footprints.

"Am I seeing things?" the officer cried out. "How did you get here? And what's going on?"

"Shortcut," Joe said. "We set up a roadblock and stopped Latsky, but he ran away."

Swinging the bright beams of their flashlights in the woods, the trio followed the footprints. They led to a wide brook.

"Latsky's clever," Chief Collig remarked. "He must have entered the water and walked either up- or downstream."

The Hardys offered to take one direction while the chief took the other, but Collig shook his head. "We'll never pick up his trail in the dark. I'll send out an alert on the radio."

The three left the woods. While Collig went ahead to phone, the Hardys paused to look over the wreck of Latsky's car.

"He dropped the cutlass!" Joe cried out suddenly as his flashlight reflected on the shining steel blade.

Grabbing it, he hurried with Frank to the police car. Chief Collig was just concluding his conversation. He was delighted to hear that the boys had retrieved their ancient sword, then said, "My men are starting out now to track down Latsky. By the way, that wrecked car was stolen. Too bad for the owner."

Soon a tow truck arrived to haul the smashed sedan to the police garage. The Hardys said good-by to the chief, and with the cutlass, started home to give it a close examination.

After telling their mother and Aunt Gertrude that they had retrieved the weapon, Frank and Joe went directly to their laboratory over the garage. Under a powerful work lamp they quickly examined the blade. On one side was etched the name of the maker, *Montoya.*

"There's probably more," Joe said excitedly, getting out bottles of chemicals with which to clean off the metal. Every inch of the fine Damascus steel blade was inspected for other markings or hidden writing. There were none.

"The maker of this cutlass must have considered it too fine to mark," Joe said. Old as it was, the sword still had a keen edge.

Next, the handle was cleaned. Every seed pearl in the design was intact, and the gold leaf was still in place.

"Let's examine that handle closely," Frank suggested, getting a magnifying glass.

There was a heavy, richly encrusted leaf scroll pattern. The Hardys scrutinized this minutely to see if it concealed any gems or contraband, but without success.

"I still think there might be something in this handle," Frank said stubbornly. "Let's try that special magnifying glass of Dad's."

"Good idea!" said Joe. "I'll get it."

He ran back to the house and in a few minutes returned with the extra-powerful glass.

Frank focused it over the handle inch by inch. Suddenly his face lighted up. "Look here, Joe!" he exclaimed, pointing.

Looking through the magnifier, Joe saw a tiny line which had been cleverly worked into the leaf pattern.

With the thin blade of a knife, Frank tried to force the crack open, but it was impossible.

"Maybe there's a spring hidden somewhere in the handle," Joe suggested. "Let me try it."

Frank handed him the cutlass and Joe bent over it intently. He pressed each tiny leaf but the crack did not widen.

"A spring could be connected with the blade," Frank mused. "But how?"

"Perhaps the spring is rusted after all these years," Joe said. "I'll try hitting the blade on something."

He looked around the laboratory and found a slab of stone left over from a previous experiment. Grasping the handle of the cutlass firmly, he jabbed the tip against the hard surface.

Click! The crack widened a full inch!

The boys were jubilant. Frank bent down and examined the sword.

"The tip contains a tiny mechanism," he said after a moment's scrutiny. "It must extend through the blade all the way to the handle. Very ingenious!"

He inspected the opening and reached into it with his thumb and forefinger.

"Anything there?" Joe asked.

"Wait a minute—"

There was a soft crinkling noise. "I can feel something," Frank said. "Here it comes."

Gingerly he pulled out a small piece of ancient parchment. It was folded up into a compact wad.

Frank carefully smoothed it out. "There's writing on it!" he exclaimed excitedly.

CHAPTER XVII

Gunner's Tools

"FRANK, this message is written in what seems to me ancient Spanish," Joe said. "I can't make it out."

"Whatever it says must be mighty important," Frank concluded, "or the writer wouldn't have hidden the message."

"And Bowden and Gorman and Latsky must think so too," Joe added.

Happy but weary, the boys went to bed, the cutlass safely tucked under Frank's mattress.

At breakfast the next morning they showed the old parchment to their mother and Aunt Gertrude. All were bending over it excitedly when Chet walked in.

"Wow!" he said when he heard the newest development in the mystery. "You sure are good detectives."

At that moment the phone rang. "I'll take it," Joe offered, hoping the caller would be Mr. Hardy.

The other boys followed him to the phone and stood near as he spoke.

Placing his hand over the mouthpiece, Joe whispered to Chet and Frank, "It's Bowden!"

He held the receiver a distance from his ear to let them hear the conversation. Bowden said that Gorman had been arrested in St. Louis while traveling under an assumed name.

"A friend of mine on the St. Louis police force, knowing I was interested, just phoned me," Bowden continued. "I guess we can go about locating the cannon without any interference from Gorman."

The boys were skeptical of the story.

To Bowden, Joe merely said, "Thank you for the information. We're working hard on the case."

The man told Joe he would let the Hardys know if anything further developed. He was about to hang up when Chet burst out:

"Tell him we've found the clue in the cutlass!"

Frank gave Chet a warning look, but too late. Bowden's next words were, "I heard what someone just said. What's it all about?"

"Oh, nothing, really," Joe replied. "Just a story we heard and haven't had time to check out yet."

"Oh." Bowden seemed to be thinking hard, but did not pursue the matter.

After Joe hung up, Chet apologized for revealing the news. Frank and Joe were disturbed but assured him that by working fast they would get to the bottom of the mystery and no harm would result from Chet's slip.

"Now if we could only think of someone who might translate the message on the parchment," Frank said.

"Let's try our Spanish teacher, Miss Kelly," Joe suggested. "If she—"

At that moment the doorbell rang. Aunt Gertrude went to answer it and presently came back with a telegram.

"It's for you," she said and handed the message over to Frank.

"From Dad," the boy said as he unfolded the telegram. "And, Joe, it's in code!"

"Let's go upstairs and decipher it," Joe said. The Hardys dashed to their father's study and removed Mr. Hardy's code book from his filing cabinet. Quickly they decoded the message:

BEWARE DOUBLE-CROSSING BY BOWDEN!

"Double-crossing!" Frank echoed the warning in the telegram. "Dad must have further information about Bowden."

"I wish he had told us more," Joe said as they returned to the front door with the news of Mr.

Hardy's message. Instantly Mrs. Hardy and Aunt Gertrude became alarmed.

The boys, fearful that their mother might insist they abandon their sleuthing, promised to take extra precautions from now on.

"If Bowden still doesn't suspect that we mistrust him," Frank said, "we'll have the advantage."

"Which we hope to hold until Dad returns," Joe added.

Chet whistled. "Well, count me out of any more trouble," he said. "I'm off for home. Let me know what that foreign parchment says, will you?"

After Chet had chugged off in his jalopy, Frank suggested that they call on Miss Kelly to see if she could translate the message found in the cutlass.

"Let's stop at police headquarters on the way," Joe said. "We'll check Bowden's story about Gorman's arrest."

With the parchment tucked securely in Frank's inner pocket, they drove to headquarters. There the sergeant in charge promised to check with St. Louis about the alleged arrest. Before leaving, Frank asked if the man named Guinness who had exploded the fireworks had been caught. The officer shook his head.

"Please let us know what you find out about Gorman," Joe said as they walked out.

Frank drove across Bayport to the small cottage where Miss Kelly lived. She was a pleasant middle-aged woman, well liked by her students.

"We wondered if you could help us solve a mystery," Joe said as they all sat down in her cool, attractive living room.

"By the expressions on your faces I thought you must be working on one," Miss Kelly said.

Frank produced the parchment. "Is this Spanish, and can you translate it?"

The teacher studied the scrawled writing for a moment. "No," she said. "This is written in Portuguese, old-fashioned Portuguese at that. But I believe Mrs. Vasquez might be able to help you."

Handing back the paper, she explained that Mrs. Vasquez was an elderly Portuguese woman, the mother of a fishing boat captain.

"She isn't well and doesn't get up until afternoon," Miss Kelly said, "but I'm sure if you go see her after lunch, she would help you. I'll give you her address."

She looked in the telephone directory and wrote it down. The boys thanked her and left.

"If we can't get the message translated until after lunch," Joe said, "let's go out to Pirates' Hill and call on Sergeant Tilton. Maybe he can give us some idea of where to dig."

"Okay," Frank agreed. "We haven't had any luck ourselves."

"This here's a gunner's scraper," Tilton replied

They drove to Tilton's cottage. The sergeant, dressed in dungarees and a coonskin cap, was working in his small flower garden.

He was in high spirits. "Hi there, boys!" he yelled.

"Good morning, Sergeant Tilton," Frank replied. "We've come to do some more digging for that cannon."

"We thought maybe you could show us where you think it should be," Joe added.

"Well, now, let me see," the man drawled as he came toward them. "Suppose I walk around the place with you." He grabbed up a folding canvas chair.

When they had gone about fifty yards along the dunes, he stopped and scratched his head. "Accordin' to my system of reckonin', the gun must have been located just about— No." He moved a few steps to his left. "Just about here."

Sergeant Tilton lighted an old pipe and seated himself comfortably on his folding chair, and the boys started digging. He told them story after story of his Army adventures while they spaded deep through the white sand.

"Hold everything!" Joe called some time later. He was standing waist-deep in a hole. "I've found something!"

He bent over and came up with a queer-looking gadget. "What would this be?" he asked, handing it to the sergeant.

Tilton examined it carefully. "This here's a gunner's scraper," he replied.

"Probably belonged to the same gear as that pick Chet found the other day," Frank whispered to Joe.

Protected by the sand, the scraper had withstood the ravages of time better than the pick had.

"The cannon's just *got* to be near here!" Joe declared excitedly.

"That's right, my boy." Tilton wore a knowing look as he gave the scraper back to Joe and resumed puffing on his pipe. "Don't stop diggin', lads." He blew out a small cloud of smoke.

Ten minutes later Frank spaded loose a six-foot-long wooden pole fixed at one end with an iron blade. As he handed it to Tilton, the old sergeant exclaimed, "It's a handspike! You must be gettin' close!"

CHAPTER XVIII

Guarding a Discovery

THOUGH eager to continue the search, Frank and Joe paused a moment.

"What was that strange-looking pole used for?" Frank asked Sergeant Tilton.

"To manhandle the heavy cannon," he replied. "With this tool, the gunners could move the carriage, or lift the breech of the gun, so they could adjust the elevatin' screw."

Jubilantly expectant, the Hardys dug deeper into the sand. But nothing further came to light.

Finally Frank straightened up. "Joe," he said, "it's noon. We'd better let our search go for now. You know we have an errand in town."

Joe had almost forgotten their plan to call on Mrs. Vasquez and have the parchment translated. "You're right, Frank." He asked Sergeant Tilton to keep the spike and pole until the boys

called for them. Then they quickly covered the
hole with branches and sand, took their tools,
and started back.

After stopping for a quick lunch, the Hardys
drove directly to Mrs. Vasquez's home. Her
daughter-in-law answered their knock, and when
Frank explained the boys' mission, they were
ushered inside.

A white-haired old lady with black eyes stared
curiously at them from a rocking chair. She
smiled, adjusted her black shawl, and motioned
for them to be seated.

"Mother doesn't speak much English," the
daughter-in-law said, "but I'll translate."

The Vasquezes spoke rapidly in Portuguese,
then the old lady leaned back in her rocking
chair and read the parchment. When she looked
up, more words in Portuguese followed.

"Mama says this message gives directions."

"For what?" Frank's heart pounded.

Again there was a rapid exchange, then the
younger woman smiled. "Directions to a cannon.
I'll write it all down."

As Mrs. Vasquez spoke, her daughter-in-law
translated and wrote:

*On high rock Alaqua Cove due east setting sun
first day July is treasure cannon. Demiculverin.*

The younger woman smiled. "Does this mean
anything to you? Where is Alaqua Cove?"

"That was an old Indian name for Bayport, I

think," Frank replied. "Thanks a million. And, please, will you keep this a secret?"

"Oh, yes. Mama and I will say nothing. I'm glad we could help you."

Frank and Joe said good-by and left the house. They were grinning ecstatically.

"At last we're going to solve this mystery!" Joe said.

"And the time of year is perfect," Frank added. "We're only about a week over the designated date. That shouldn't give us much trouble."

On reaching Pirates' Hill with their digging tools, Joe became restless. "I hate to wait until sunset. Can't we start?"

"Sure. We've been here so much the past few days I can tell you exactly where the sun has been setting."

Frank pointed to a distant church spire. "Right there." He took a compass from his pocket and moved about until his back was due east of the spire. "The cannon should be somewhere along this line," he said and shuffled through the sand.

"The directions said 'high rock,'" Joe reminded him. "There are rocks under the sand. Let's try the highest point on this line."

The boys set to work. All afternoon they dug furiously. Finally, as the sun was about to set, Frank's spade struck metal!

"Joe," he cried, "this must be it!"

A moment later they uncovered the curve of a barrel, and judging from its dimensions, they were convinced that this was the Spanish demi-culverin for which they had been searching.

"Success!" Frank exclaimed.

Then suddenly he sobered. "We'd better be careful," he said. "Somebody might be spying on us."

"You're right," Joe agreed. "Let's cover up the gun again. It's getting dark and we won't be able to dig the whole thing up tonight."

Shoveling quickly they concealed the valuable discovery until they could come back the next day and uncover it completely. Then, to bewilder any prying eyes, the Hardys decided to make small excavations at other spots.

A short time later two figures appeared over the dunes. Tony Prito and Chet!

"We came out in the *Napoli*," Tony said. "Figured you'd be here. We called your house and your mother gave us a message for you."

"About Gorman," Chet added. "The police left word that he's not in St. Louis."

"Just as we suspected," Joe said.

Then Frank, in a low voice, told about finding the demiculverin. "Wow!" Chet exploded.

Tony congratulated his friends and asked what their next move would be.

"We'll dig up the whole cannon tomorrow," Frank replied.

"I sure wish we could stay here tonight and get an early start," Joe said. "Say, why don't we camp out and stand guard over the cannon?"

"Swell idea," Frank agreed.

Tony offered to go back in the Hardys' car and pick up a tent, sleeping bags, and food.

"I'll call your folks and tell them," he promised.

Two hours later the camp on Pirates' Hill was ready, with the tent pitched on the cannon site. As the stars came out, the Hardys and Chet crawled into their shelter. Tony had volunteered to stand guard first and posted himself outside the tent flap.

At eleven o'clock he became aware of an approaching figure. Instantly he awoke his sleeping pals. They waited tensely until the person was almost within reach.

"Get him!" Joe cried suddenly.

The campers lunged out of the shelter. Just as Joe was about to tackle the figure, he recognized him.

"Sergeant Tilton!" he exclaimed.

"So it's you," drawled the elderly man. He explained that he had spotted their flashlights and had come to see who his neighbors were.

Knowing that the sergeant was inclined to gossip, the boys decided to keep their finding of the cannon to themselves. They chatted casually with Tilton, telling him they had set up camp to be ready for some sleuthing early in the morning.

"Well," the sergeant said finally, "I reckon I'd better git back to my shack. I suspect you'll all be snorin' soon." He chuckled and walked off.

The rest of the night passed quietly, with the boys rotating the guard watches as they had planned earlier. By six o'clock they were up and preparing breakfast. After eating, the Hardys and Tony started work under the tent, with Chet acting as lookout.

Within an hour the three had dug a deep pit and uncovered the entire demiculverin. The old fieldpiece appeared to be in good condition.

"What a beauty!" Frank exclaimed.

"And look at this number on it!" Joe cried out. Engraved on the barrel were the numerals 8–4–20. "It must be a code for this type. Let's find out what it stands for."

Leaving Chet and Tony on guard, the Hardys went home in the convertible to check through their father's books on cannons. Joe's hunch that the numerals might be a code led to nothing. They read on.

Suddenly Frank exclaimed, "I get it! An eight-pound ball and four pounds of powder."

"And twenty degrees of elevation!" Joe beamed.

Hearing the excited conversation of the boys, Mrs. Hardy looked into the room and asked, "Have you found out something interesting?"

"Sunken treasure!" Joe exulted. "A ball shot from the demiculverin probably marks the spot where the old merchantman was sunk by the pirates in that Battle of Bayport!"

Mrs. Hardy was astounded. She started to praise her sons when the front doorbell rang. Frank hurried down to answer it. Opening the door, he blinked in amazement.

Bowden!

As Frank recovered from his surprise, he said, "Come in," and called loudly over his shoulder, "Joe! Mr. Bowden's here!"

Joe came down the stairs like a streak of lightning. "What's up now?" he wondered.

Bowden smiled. "Can't stay but a few minutes. Good news travels fast. I understand you've located the cannon I asked you to find!"

The Hardys were dumbfounded.

"I'll have the money for you shortly for solving my case," Bowden continued. "And I'll send a truck out to Pirates' Hill tomorrow to pick up the demiculverin."

CHAPTER XIX

Human Targets

FRANK and Joe were speechless for a moment. Then Frank asked, "How did you hear we found a cannon?"

The man's reply proved to be another bombshell. "I was out there and your friends told me."

Frank's mind whirled. He looked at Joe and realized his brother was thinking the same thing. Whatever Bowden's real reason was for wanting the ancient cannon, they were going to keep it from him until further word arrived from their father or the police.

Bowden again seemed to be one step ahead of them. "You don't know it yet, but I own Pirates' Hill."

"What?" Frank asked, thunderstruck.

Bowden pulled several documents from his pocket. One was a certificate of sale, another a government release, and the third a letter with a notary-public seal. This stated that Bowden had a right to anything found on Pirates' Hill.

"They certainly look authentic," Frank said, but realized the papers could be clever forgeries.

Mr. Hardy's warning to his sons indicated that Bowden was probably a confidence man. It was possible that he had accomplices who could imitate signatures and print fake documents.

"I must get in touch with Dad about this," Frank said to himself.

He and Joe knew that the only course was not to let Bowden know of their suspicions. But Joe winced as his brother spoke.

"It looks as if the hill is yours all right, Mr. Bowden. If there's a cannon on it, there may be other treasures, too."

Frank's assurance pleased Bowden. "I hope you're right. And I'm glad you see the whole thing my way. To tell the truth, I thought you might want the old cannon yourselves. Accept my congratulations for a grand job."

After he left, Frank said, "I'll bet those papers Bowden showed us are fake!"

Joe nodded. "We'd better let Dad know about this right away."

Since it was not possible to reach Mr. Hardy by telephone, they composed a telegram in code, mentioning the fact that the cannon had been found and Bowden was claiming it. Frank phoned the message to the telegraph office.

"I hope this information will bring Dad up here," Joe said. "Bowden is crooked, Frank. We can't just hand him the cannon."

"Of course not. But don't forget, Joe, digging out the sand around the demiculverin so it can be lifted, and lugging the two tons of iron over the sand may take days. Maybe something will happen in the meantime to stop Bowden."

"Let's hope so," said Joe. "Well, how about doing some computing on those numbers we found on the cannon?"

"Good thought." The boys quickly discovered, however, that they were unable to solve the gunnery problem. Frank suggested that they drive over to see Mr. Rowe, head of the Mathematics Department at Bayport High. "He's teaching summer school. I'm sure he'll be there now."

They set off for Bayport High and found Mr. Rowe. Intrigued by the problem, he went to work, filling several sheets of paper with calculations. At last he said:

"The cannon ball would land two thousand yards away, if trained and elevated at precisely the angle given in my figures."

Frank and Joe thanked him, then hurried to their car. On the way back to Pirates' Hill, Frank remarked that if the demiculverin had not been moved, and currents had not shifted the ship, the treasure should be easy to locate.

Joe grinned. "Let's measure two thousand

yards from the cannon, then hand it over to Bowden with our compliments!"

Frank reminded his brother that whatever their plans, they had to work fast. He parked off the shore road as before and the Hardys ran up to Chet and Tony.

Suddenly Joe stopped short. Grabbing Frank by the arm, he cried out, "Look! There's Bowden again!"

At the site of the cannon, Bowden and Sergeant Tilton were talking to Chet and Tony.

"Good-by to our plan," Joe said.

"Maybe not," Frank remarked. "It might take him some time to catch on to the whole thing."

Chet and Tony dashed up to meet the boys and whispered that after Frank and Joe had gone back to town, they had continued digging. The two men had caught them off guard.

"You can see the cannon very plainly now," Tony said. "We thought we'd surprise you and remove all the sand from the front of it."

"Thanks," Joe said. "It was a nice idea."

Frank quickly related Bowden's visit to the house. Tony frowned. "Maybe that gossipy Sergeant Tilton told him we were here."

As the group reached the men, the Hardys received only a nod from Bowden, but the genial old sergeant began to talk excitedly. He explained that at Bowden's request he was preparing a charge similar to the one he used to test the mortar in the town square at Bayport.

In spite of Bowden's efforts to signal him to keep quiet, Tilton continued, "An' I'm goin' to test the strength o' the barrel fer Mr. Bowden. He wants to be sure it'll be safe fer him to fire off durin' that there exposition in Florida."

"Are you sure you aren't planning to shoot a cannon ball?" Joe asked suspiciously.

The old gunner protested in disgust. "Of course not. That'd be against the law. I'd have to git permission from the Coast Guard."

"That's right," said Joe, eying Bowden to watch his reaction. But the man showed none.

As the boys looked on, Tilton prepared the powder charge and fired the gun. A thunderous boom followed. As the smoke cleared, he rushed back to inspect the cannon.

"She stood up fine!" he exclaimed.

"Well, thanks, Sergeant," said Bowden. "I guess the cannon will do for the pageant. I'll see you later," he added as he walked away.

The old man began running his hands along the cannon and talking to himself. "Great piece o' work," he declared. He turned to Frank and Joe. "I'd like to tell you a bit about this."

"We'd like to hear it a little later," said Frank.

The Hardys were eager to locate the old

sunken merchantman. When their friends agreed to help, Frank asked Chet to drive to their boat-house in the convertible to pick up the aqualung diving gear. Tony offered the use of the *Napoli* from which to work.

When Chet reached the road, Bowden was just driving away. As his car gathered speed Chet saw a piece of paper blow out the window. Pick-ing it up, he examined it curiously.

"Why, it's a stock certificate of the Copper Slope Mining Company. It must be valuable," he mused. "I'd better return it to Bowden."

Suddenly he recalled what Frank and Joe had told him about Bowden selling stock to a man in Taylorville. "This certificate might be phony!"

Chet decided to leave the certificate at the Hardys' home for inspection later on. He got into the convertible and drove to Bayport.

Out on Pirates' Hill, Frank was saying to the old sergeant, "Now tell us about this cannon."

Tilton beamed. "Firing a gun like this here one is a pretty risky thing."

He went on to explain that the demiculverin most likely had been used at some Spanish co-lonial fort before the pirates had captured it. The normal life of such a cannon was twelve hundred rounds. But at an outpost, where it was hard to get new weapons, a piece was always fired many rounds beyond that figure, increasing the danger of explosion with each burst.

"When cracks develop 'round the vent or in the bore," Tilton said, "you got to be careful. The muzzle sometimes blows clean off 'em!"

Digging away more sand, the boys found that the cannon was mounted on a mahogany four-wheeled truck carriage used on eighteenth-century ships and garrison guns. It was covered with beautiful leaf designs, wrought in iron.

"Look!" Joe cried. "It's chained to a boulder."

This convinced the Hardys that they had been right in their deductions. The cannon was placed so that a ball fired from it would strike one particular place in the ocean!

The boys took sights along the gun barrel and checked them with their compass. The barrel pointed due east. This would make it easy to estimate the approximate spot where the treasure should be. They chafed under the necessity of awaiting Chet's return.

"What you fellows aimin' to do, now that you got this mystery solved?" Tilton asked them.

"Look for another case, I guess," Joe replied. "Right now we're going for a swim." To himself he added, "And look for the buried treasure!"

"Hm!" said Tilton. "I ain't been in the water fer nigh onto thirty years."

He climbed off the gun emplacement just as Chet came hurrying across the sand without the diving gear.

"Something's up!" Joe declared.

Puffing, Chet halted. "Frank—Joe, I've got big news. Chief Collig phoned your home. Latsky's been captured!"

"Honestly?" Frank exclaimed, hardly daring to believe it was true.

"Great!" Joe cried out. "How?"

"He finally returned to the cabin. Seems he had money buried near there and had run out of funds," Chet replied. "The police had no trouble nabbing him."

Joe grinned. "Latsky'll be back in the penitentiary for a long stretch."

After a brief discussion about him, Frank looked at Chet. "In all the excitement I guess you forgot our diving gear."

Chet laughed and told him it was in the car. The boys said good-by to Tilton and went to pick up the equipment. On the way Chet told the others about the stock certificate Bowden had lost and that Mrs. Hardy now had it.

"Swell work, Chet!" Frank exclaimed.

The diving gear was carried to the beach. As the boys waded out to the *Napoli,* Joe reviewed what they would do. Tony and Chet were to remain aboard the boat, while Frank and Joe did the diving.

"We'll work by dead reckoning on the first attempt," Joe told his pals. "Frank and I will go over the side at the estimated distance from the shore."

"Let's get started," Tony urged.

"Hold on!" Frank said. "I think we're foolish to leave the cannon unguarded with Bowden loose. No telling what he may try to pull."

"What do you suggest?" Joe asked.

"That one of us go back and watch. If Bowden comes, our guard can signal and we'll get to the hill in a hurry."

"I'll do it," Chet offered. "But how?"

Tony took a large yellow bandanna and a clean white rag out of the boat's locker. He handed them to Chet. "Wigwag with these," he said.

"And be sure to hide behind a dune," Frank cautioned, "so Bowden won't see you."

The others climbed into the motorboat and Tony started the engine. Frank and Joe gave directions to the site of the sunken treasure, using the church spire as a landmark and keeping on a course due east. Tony steered the *Napoli* carefully while Frank and Joe tried to estimate a distance of two thousand yards from shore.

"Stop!" Frank commanded presently. "Unless all our reckoning is wrong, the treasure ship must be directly below us."

There was silence for a few moments as the full import of Frank's words struck them all. They might be about to make an intriguing find!

"Let's go down!" Joe urged his brother.

The Hardys donned their gear and climbed over the side.

Tony, watching Chet intently, suddenly cried out, "Wait, fellows! Chet is signaling!"

Back on Pirates' Hill their pal had seen Bowden sneaking up to the cannon. As he watched the man, terror struck his heart. Bowden was ramming a charge of powder into the ancient gun. Then he inserted a cannon ball into the muzzle!

All this time Chet was wigwagging. The boys on the water interpreted, *"Bowden here. Look out for—"*

The missile ready, Bowden ran to the back of the cannon and inserted a fuse into the vent hole. Chet's hands were shaking with fright. Bowden flicked on his lighter and held it to the fuse, then stepped back.

"Run!" Chet signaled.

Boom!

With a shuddering detonation the demi-culverin sent the deadly ball directly toward the *Napoli!*

CHAPTER XX

Divers' Reward

WHAM! *Smack!*

The cannon ball hit the *Napoli* a second after the boys had flung themselves away from it. Spray and debris flew in every direction.

The Hardys, only a few feet away, were knocked unconscious by the concussion. Tony, unhurt, was worried about his companions. He realized that in their diving equipment they would float and could breathe even if they were unconscious. However, he was afraid that his friends might not have survived the shock.

Catching up to Joe, he was just in time to see the boy move his arms. He was alive!

"Thank goodness!" Tony said to himself. Then he went to find Frank. To his relief, he too had regained consciousness. Frank removed the mouthpiece of the air hose and took a deep breath.

"Do you think Bowden meant to kill us?" Tony asked.

"It certainly looks that way."

Just then Joe swam over to them. One glance at the *Napoli* told the three boys that it was doomed.

"Too bad," said Joe.

"Guess we'll have to swim to shore. Stick close to us, Tony," Frank advised.

The boys struck out toward the distant beach, but they had not swum fifty yards when they heard the roar of a motor.

"A Coast Guard boat!" Joe called out.

The launch circled to pick them up. The young lieutenant in charge, Ted Newgate, was glad to see that they were all right.

"We heard the report of a cannon and came to investigate," he said as they were hauled aboard. "What's going on here?"

"Someone on the hill tried to blow us out of the water," Joe answered. "I want to get to shore as fast as possible and find him."

The powerful motor kicked up foam as the boat headed toward land. Nearing Pirates' Hill, Frank gave a cry. "Joe, there's Dad on the beach with Chief Collig and Chet."

Joe shaded his eyes. "And look who's handcuffed to Collig! Bowden!"

Quickly the boys told the lieutenant about the secret of Pirates' Hill. The young man was amazed and congratulated them on their good work. Then he put them ashore in the launch's gig. When the bow hit the sand, Frank and Joe raced across the beach to greet their father, a handsome man in his early forties.

"Are you all right?" he asked.

"We're okay, Dad, but no thanks to Bowden," Frank replied.

The police chief said, "You can thank your lucky stars you're still here to tell the story. The charge against Bowden will be assault and battery with intent to kill. And the Coast Guard will have something to say about his firing without permission."

Bowden looked completely beaten. The police chief explained that the man had stolen a cannon ball from the town square, hoping to use it to locate the sunken merchantman.

"When he spotted you fellows out there, Bowden saw a good chance to eliminate you from the race for the treasure."

Joe glared at the prisoner. "We didn't trust you, but we didn't think you were a killer."

"If the repercussion from that old cannon hadn't knocked him out, he would have got away before your dad and I showed up," Collig stated. "He was armed, so Chet wouldn't have had a chance to stop him. Well, Bowden will get a long stretch in prison to pay for his crimes."

Frank asked his father how he happened to

have come to Pirates' Hill. "Because I hoped Bowden was here and I wanted to have him arrested for selling fake stock certificates." Mr. Hardy smiled broadly. "You've helped me solve my own case of bringing a notorious gang of swindlers to justice. I've been tracking this fellow's friends all over the South. They've been counterfeiting stock, getting prospective customers through the mail and selling them phony certificates."

Joe inquired when Mr. Hardy had arrived from Florida. "Only an hour ago," the detective said. "When your telegram came, I flew up. Chet clinched matters by leaving the stock certificate that had blown out of Bowden's car. The instant your mother handed it to me I recognized it as a counterfeit."

Hearing this, the prisoner winced, chagrined to think that he had given himself away by carelessly losing the document.

Collig started to walk toward the shore road. "We'd better get this man behind bars."

The others followed. When they reached the police car, the chief phoned headquarters to report he had a prisoner. In turn the sergeant on duty reported that he was holding a suspect for the Hardy boys to identify.

"Follow me in your car," Collig directed.

On their arrival at police headquarters, Frank

and Joe were first shown a black skin-diving suit and a yellow-trimmed skull cap.

"The spearman that shot at us wore gear like this!" Joe cried out. "Sergeant, where did you get it?"

"From that man over there—Guinness."

The Hardys turned to look. "The guy who shot rockets at us Fourth of July!" Frank exclaimed. "Say, Guinness, how did you know we were going to be there that night?"

Collig informed both prisoners that they did not have to answer any questions, and advised them of their constitutional rights. But Guinness decided to talk.

"I didn't," he said, "but my chance came right then and I took it."

Guinness admitted he was in league with Latsky, whom he had met recently. But the prisoner denied knowing Bowden or anyone named Gorman.

"What about the paper with the name Smedick on it which the police found in your wastebasket?" Frank asked. "Didn't you know Smedick was Gorman?"

Guinness said No, but thought Latsky must have discovered Gorman's alias and dropped the paper on one of his visits to Guinness's room.

"Where is Gorman?" Frank shot at Bowden.

The man did not answer, but this fact gave

Frank a lead. As events flashed through his mind, an idea came to him.

"You had Gorman attacked at the rear of the beach shack and taken away. Later, you hid him in the trunk compartment of your car. We heard him moan!"

Bowden's face went ashen. Frank's surmise had turned the tide. Bowden confessed that he had lied to the boys about Gorman's character. He had had him trailed and ambushed at the shack by henchmen. When the Hardys arrived unexpectedly, it had been necessary for the thugs to attack them, too. Worried, they had taken the young detectives to the gully and dumped them. Then they had abandoned the car.

Upon their return to the shack the henchmen had met Bowden and told the story. Later, Bowden had driven past the gully to check and received a real surprise.

"I had to rescue you because I wanted you to think it was on the level," Bowden said. "That moan you heard in my car was Gorman. I told you it had been made by the wind."

"Where is Gorman now?" Frank demanded.

"You'll find him in the room next to mine at the motel, tied up. He's supposed to be sick and has an attendant. No one else goes in," Bowden said.

Chief Collig sent two men immediately to release Gorman. While the others waited, more facts were revealed about the case.

During a prison term at the Delmore penitentiary, Bowden, whose real name was Bell, had met Latsky who knew a great deal about ancient cannon, including the story of the Battle of Bayport. Each man was determined to find the treasure for himself after being released. It became a bitter race, with Gorman against both of them.

"First you had to locate the cutlass with the directions," said Frank.

"Yes," Bowden admitted. "Latsky tried to steal the swords from the Bayport Historical Society but failed. Then I took them."

"I see. And when you found none of them contained the parchment, you had Gil Fanning sell them. Latsky later bought the five cutlasses but could not locate the clue either."

"And you had Chet lured off to be questioned and slugged him. Then you put him in the gully with Frank and me," Joe said.

As he was talking, two officers walked in with Gorman and an eighteen-year-old youth.

Chet gazed in amazement. "That's the fellow who led me into a trap!" he exclaimed.

The new prisoner was identified as Gil Fanning, who had been Gorman's attendant at the motel. He had needed money, so he agreed to work for Bowden.

"I—I didn't think I was doing anything wrong," Gil said. "Then first thing I knew, I was in so deep I couldn't get out."

Bowden admitted that the boy had been his dupe, and hoped that harsh punishment would not be meted out to him. The ex-convict then revealed the names of his henchmen, and Chief Collig ordered their immediate arrest.

The Hardys turned to Gorman and asked if he felt all right. "Yes," he replied, "and I'm glad you boys uncovered the secret in the cutlass, instead of Latsky and Bowden."

He told them that the directions to the cannon, according to the legend, had been hidden in the cutlass belonging to the pirates' captain. Along with five other swords it had been given to someone in the Bayport area for safekeeping.

Gorman had learned about the treasure and the demiculverin from an ancient diary. "It was written by the wife of the merchantman's captain. She tried for years to locate the site of her husband's sunken ship."

Gorman said he was a direct descendant of the captain and that the diary was his property. After his discharge from the Navy he decided to look for the treasure site.

"Which I never would have discovered if you boys hadn't found the cannon, and Mr. Hardy and the chief hadn't caught Bowden," Gorman said.

"It was probably Latsky," Joe said, "who threatened Bowden in the message we found on his door and who subsequently sent us a threat."

Bowden confirmed this. "He later knocked me out when I was talking to you fellows on the phone."

"Who was hiding under the tarpaulin in the boat when Halpen warned us away from the sting ray?" Frank asked.

"I was," Guinness replied. "Latsky had hired me to dive for the sunken treasure ship. When you showed up one morning, I thought you were hunting, too. So I shot a couple of spears at you to scare you off."

Joe whistled. "When I saw that first spear coming, I had no idea that Frank and I would be involved in an undersea treasure hunt!"

When the questioning ended, the prisoners were led away and the others left. Mr. Hardy invited Gorman to stay at their home until he had recovered completely.

"And please forgive Joe and me for suspecting you," Frank said.

"I will on one condition," Gorman replied with a grin. "That you show me where that treasure is and let me share with you whatever the government will let us have."

The Hardys laughed and Joe said, "That won't be hard to take!"

"But first," said Frank, "from whatever we

get, I suggest that we buy Tony a new and even better *Napoli*."

The others quickly agreed, then Joe said, "I guess this treasure hunt will be the most exciting adventure we've ever had."

But another was soon to come their way, which was to become known as *The Ghost at Skeleton Rock*.

Two days later the whole group, in skin-diving outfits, climbed over the side of the *Sleuth* and descended to a depth of thirty feet at the same spot they had been fired on by Bowden. There lay the ancient merchantman, its timbers rotted away, and moss and barnacles covering the metal parts.

Cautiously Gorman and the boys swam in and out, removing the debris. At last their search was rewarded. There, in the uncovered hold of the old vessel, lay a vast quantity of gold bullion. Through their masks, the divers beamed at one another triumphantly.

The Hardys and their friends had found the ancient treasure!

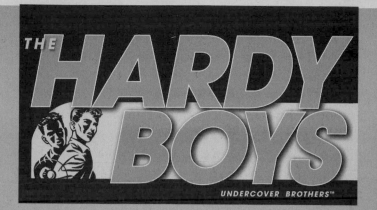

Match Wits with The Hardy Boys®!

Collect the Complete
Hardy Boys Mystery Stories®
by Franklin W. Dixon

The Hardy Boys Back-to-Back

Celebrate over 70 Years with the World's Greatest Super Sleuths!

Match Wits with Super Sleuth Nancy Drew!

Collect the Complete
Nancy Drew Mystery Stories®
by Carolyn Keene

Celebrate over 70 years with the World's Best Detective